ONE RECKLESS SUMMER

DANI WYATT

Copyright © 2024
by Dani Wyatt

All rights reserved. This book or any portion thereof
may not be reproduced or used in any manner whatsoever
without the express written permission of the publisher
except for the use of brief quotations in a book review.
This is a work of fiction. Names, characters, businesses, places,
events and incidents are either the products
of the author's imagination
or used in a fictitious manner.
Any resemblance to actual persons, living or dead,
is purely coincidental.

www.daniwyatt.com

DEDICATION

A NOTE TO MY READERS:
I appreciate every one of you.

If he will burn down the house to
Make sure the spider is dead...
He's a keeper.

VIP'S

GET exclusive free books and other bonus epilogues and short stores by joining the reader's group!

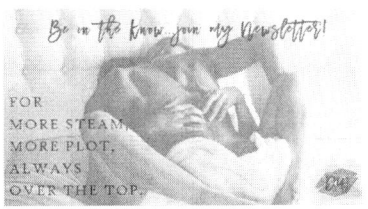

NEWSLETTER

Chapter One

Summer

"Licking salt off my hand is going to help how, exactly?" I stare down at the shot glass, already dreading tomorrow morning.

"Here's to bad decisions!" My best friend Dolly clinks her glass to mine, licks the side of her hand, tosses back the tequila and sucks on the lime in one fluid motion.

She slams the shot glass down on the black laminate high top with a resounding crack, raising her fists in victory and drawing the eyes of every man in this north of nowhere bar as she swipes the backs of her fingers over her plum-colored lips.

"*Yeeeeeehawwwww!*" She yelps, shaking her head

while sucking air through her teeth. "That'll wake ya up in the mornin' boys, won't it?"

Dolly draws attention wherever she goes, with legs to her neck, a jet-black Uma Thurman circa Pulp Fiction bob, and a face that could launch a thousand bar fights. But here in Ompotomic, Michigan, where they are more bears than people?

Every guy here must be thinking they're not in Kansas anymore.

Neon beer signs and horrible fluorescent lighting give everything in here an odd green glow, and there is clearly no regular cleaning schedule for the restrooms.

And don't get me started on the floors. It's like walking on the sticky side of duct tape.

"What are you waiting for?" She rounds her mouth, squinting one eye at the trembling tequila shot I'm holding a few inches in front of my lips.

"Christmas?" I suggest, screwing up my mouth on an unsteady exhale.

"Well, Santa's coming down your chimney right now." She smiles, easing the glass toward my lips. "Lick, swallow, suck," she says on a snort. "That's not *always* the right order, but with tequila *it is*. You're the one who wanted a reckless summer before we start adulting for real next year. Don't pussy out on me now."

She tosses a wink at the two ruddy-looking farmers sitting at the table next to us, as I shake my head, looking up at the bowing, water-stained ceiling tile above our table.

She's right, I did ask her to join me in one last frivolous choice before we head in our different directions this September. That choice turned out to be Camp WanderLust, a wilderness adventure park in the wilds of Michigan's Upper Peninsula where she's been a counselor since our freshman year at Michigan State.

She said it's been taken over by some new high-adrenaline adventure type, and this will be the last summer for kids to attend. There was some nostalgia there for her, so I signed on, making her promise me she would sweep my cabin twice a day for spiders.

Besides, getting as far away from my ex as possible in a place with limited to no cell service made Dolly's proposition more appealing.

Still, I'm a fish out of water here, and I haven't even gotten to the camp yet. The only stars I've ever slept under are the ones my nightlight used to project on my ceiling when I was a little girl, and my idea of roughing it is staying in a three-star hotel with no room service.

And I know there will be spiders but Dolly can talk me into almost anything.

Lick, swallow, suck, I repeat in my head, doing my best to emotionally prepare for my first tequila shot.

I do a mental countdown, 3, 2, *1*, curl my toes inside my cowboy boots, take a swipe of the salt from my hand with my tongue, and *go*.

I immediately know this is going to be a night to remember.

Or forget.

Holy shit.

My gag reflex kicks in, nearly expelling the shot all over Dolly's black AC/DC tank top before she shoves the slice of lime between my bared teeth.

"Suck!" she yells, delivering a smile to the farmers again, who haven't taken their eyes off her since we sat down.

I do as I'm told, desperate for anything to replace the taste of the poison in my mouth, as sweat breaks on my forehead and my upper lip, while a wave of heat cascades and prickles over my skin.

"Oh, *my gawd*," I choke out through the burning in my throat, fumbling my attempt to slam the shot glass onto the table like she did. It clicks against the laminate in a sad roll onto its side spinning toward the edge, where Dolly catches it on a laugh.

"Not sure I'm cut out for a reckless summer after all," I hiss, as the liquor reaches my stomach, and bile tickles the back of my throat.

How am I here? I didn't even own a backpack or a pair of hiking boots before last week.

I like manicures and lash extensions and body glitter.

Don't get me wrong. I respect the boho, quirky, 'I just never fit in' girls and the darker emo version of such as much as I support the Botox, IG, bikini wax crowd. I'm an equal opportunity queen supporter.

You do you, I'll do me and may we never disagree.

"You did *good*, girl." Dolly rubs my back as I drop my

head between my legs like they teach you to do when you think you're going to pass out.

"I almost threw up all over you," I mumble to the floor, trying to distract myself by counting the blobs of gum flattened on the sticky black linoleum.

Blood rushes through my ears, into my head, warming my cheeks as my liver sucks up the alcohol, making the world wavy around the edges.

Just as I'm starting to feel pleasantly woozy, dread returns, as my Dolly shouts, "Who wants to buy us two more?!"

This little honky-tonk bar erupts with excited male voices, as my stomach lurches, and I grip the edge of the high top, pulling myself upward. Walking on the wild side with Dolly is nothing new. You know that friend you always seem to be with when trouble comes calling?

Yeah, that's Dolly.

But for all her craziness and tough love, she has a gooey soft center and is my ride or die, one hundred percent. We met in kindergarten when Bobby Malloy was teasing me about my Hello Kitty backpack with matching shoes and lunchbox. She showed up in her black combat boots and Slenderman t-shirt and took him down with one punch, and we've been yin and yang ever since.

Willie Nelson's slow melodic drawl streams from the ancient jukebox on the side wall. An older couple probably close to eighty, wearing matching polyester baby-blue wranglers and plaid snap-up shirts, spin and sidestep on the small dance floor, alongside a handful of thirty-something women holding each other up, eyes glazed, with the one in the center wearing an "I'm the bride, again" satin sash.

The drive up to Ompotomic took twelve hours, six am to six pm, and when I got here, I crashed before the sound of Dolly banging on the door to my room at the bed and breakfast woke me from a dead sleep.

The Black Swan B & B is the best this town can manage, which isn't saying much, but for one last night of luxury it's better than nothing. The room was a pleasant enough surprise, with a squishy soft queen-sized bed, a bathroom with one of those white cast iron claw-foot tubs, and a good view of the wooded mountains that will be my home for the summer. Plus, nary a spider web was found even under the bed. And, trust me, I checked.

Dolly knows the town well from her years at the camp and she told me there's only one place where a couple of girls could kick back and have a little memorable fun.

And that's how we ended up at One Horse Earl's, dressed like cowgirl strippers. Dolly can talk me into almost anything. Including the most uncomfortable pair of Daisy Dukes ever created.

Every head turned when we walked in. I wanted to go hide in the corner, but instead Dolly draped her arm around my shoulders and sashayed us to a table in the center of the room under a spotlight that should be pointing toward the dance floor but surely got knocked off-kilter in some chair throwing brawl.

But, for all my uptight reticence, and the foul-tasting shot, I am having fun. Letting loose in a town where you know no one, and anyone you might get to know you'll never see again, has a certain freeing effect I hadn't expected.

"Here you go." The smiling waitress nods toward a couple guys slugging back long necks at the bar as she slides two whipped cream covered shots in front of us.

Outside of some White Claw and overpriced craft beer on occasion, I'm not much of a drinker, but seems tonight that's going to change.

Dolly nods, holding up one of the shots to our benefactors. One of them nods in return, clearly eye fucking her from across the room, while his friend with a clean-shaven head and dirty t-shirt looks away, more annoyed than interested.

"You get first dibs." Dolly tosses back the shot, while I opt for a fake first taste, as my brain starts to buzz. "Why wait? This place has got v-card punchers of all shapes and sizes, ready and willing to serve. You know what I say, the best way to get over an ex is to get on top of someone new."

"God, no. Not tonight." I shake my head, blowing my long bangs from my cheek, as Dolly tips the bottom of my shot glass upward.

With a hard swallow and a swipe of my hand over

my mouth, I take in the selection of men in the small space.

I push the toes of my...well, *Dolly's*...cowboy boots together, along with my knees, wondering if my summer goal of losing my virginity is such a good idea after all.

The night before I left my parents' house in Bloomfield for our camp adventure, I spent the night bingeing on rice crispy treats and Red Vines, watching all the classic summer virginity losing movies I could find.

My mom always told me she wanted to be Kristy McNichol or Tatum O'Neal when she was a teenager. Over the years, she made me watch The Bad News Bears a hundred times and Little Darlings a hundred more.

Now, here I am, a twenty-one-year-old virgin about to play out her own summer camp cherry-popping story, but from what I can tell, there's no Matt Dillon in this crowd.

It's not that I'm disinterested in sex. I have...urges.

My ex-boyfriend—slash implied fiancé—Greg would probably beg to differ on that, but I trusted my gut thank goodness, and after I found out he was skimming my bank account to support his CS'GO addiction, I found the courage to get off that ride.

That's the thing about virginity. It's a one-shot deal. If you 'give' it to someone with some emotional attachment and then, bam, you find out they're a *Greg*, it feels like you've been punked.

So I decided to lose it to someone who won't be some

long-term disappointment. This way, it can be on my terms. A hot one-night stand or a short summer fling, and that's it. No strings, no long sappy goodbyes.

No expectations.

That was the plan, at least. But the shine is fading already. Maybe I'll wait until I start my master's studies at NYU in the fall. There has to be some hot grad student in the speech therapy program that would happily take the honors.

I peel my thighs from the sticky vinyl seat cushion, adjusting myself as I grip the edge of the tabletop for support.

Our shot-buying benefactors are walking our way as Dolly shoots me a wink, leaning an elbow on the table, cocking her hip and swinging her leg forward and back, scuffing the bottom of her black cowboy boot on the linoleum floor.

"Which one do you fancy?" she hiss-whispers as they come closer. "You get first pick."

My urge to bolt toward the door clutches at my throat. I look ridiculous in this cowgirl stripper outfit. I tug at the tied-up knot on the front of my shirt, the flesh of my belly pooching out, and there are dimples on my thighs where they push against the seat. I'm happy with my body, but right now I just wish I was wearing something a little less...obvious.

The next half hour is a blur of whipped cream covered shots and awkwardly watching my best friend flirt, while the taller guy with the shaved head tells me I should smile more. I grit my teeth and stay civil, because Dolly looks like she's in hog heaven. The other guy seems genuinely interested in her and honestly is not a complete douche. He even bowed down and kissed the toe of her boot when she lifted it for him.

In another life, I think she'd have made one hell of a pro-domme.

I, on the other hand, am dreaming of a bubble bath back at the bed and breakfast, with my v-card living to see another day.

"Hey, give me a little smile." Bald guy leans his meaty forearms on the edge of the table, his entire hulking weight tipping it off balance, spilling my bag and all of our drinks onto the floor around his feet as he steps back. "Jesus, fuck! Watch what you're doing!"

His hands fly upward, spilled beer drenching the front of his jeans. His condescending sticky-sweet mask drops as anger digs into his ruddy features, red creeping over his face, making him look like a volcano ready to blow.

By this time, Dolly has transitioned to the dance-floor with baldy's friend, smiling and spinning on her cowboy boots like she's the hoedown queen of Ompotomic.

"*You* leaned on the table," I snap, hopping off my chair and dropping into a crouch in a rush to salvage the contents of my bag from the beer and whiskey dripping down from the tabletop.

I play through the excuses I could use to get away

from him—or get him to *go* away without cock blocking Dolly's good time.

I swallow down the curses gathering in my throat, as he kicks at the broken glass around his feet, slapping his hands down the front of his grimy t-shirt as I pinch the corner of my dripping wallet on a grimace and shove it inside my bag.

"You're not even my type." He scowls on a disgusted grunt. "I was just being *nice* because my friend had a hard-on for your girl."

He jerks his thumb toward the dance floor, making no effort to help me pick up the contents of my spilled bag, when a new pair of worn work boots strides into view from my left.

"That's a shitty thing to say." A low, gravelly voice that's attached to the new boots cuts through the chatter and twang of a Hank Williams song. "And pretty sure you aren't my sister's type either."

His sister?

I start to look up when my eyes catch the shimmer of three gold-foil packets lying only inches from the tip of the deep baritone guy's left boot.

Shit.

I snatch them from the floor, shifting back onto my heels, my canvas bag in one hand, the strip of three condoms in the other, intending to hide them before anyone can see, but when my gaze lifts, I freeze.

There's not just the size difference in the two men's feet, but the knees of the guy attached to the boots are a good six or eight inches higher than baldy's. I continue my visual trek north, taking in thick thighs that fill out worn denim, while further up something equally thick has a heat wave moving over my skin as the award-winning bulge challenges his zipper.

He doesn't shift when I stare, and suddenly I break out of my trance and look up to see dark eyes inspecting me from under a cinched brow. He lowers his hand with a click of his teeth. His face is hard lines and smoldering intensity, but there's a softness to his magnificent lips that I want to explore with my tongue.

"Stand up, sis, you're going to cut yourself." He moves his tongue around the inside of his cheek, flicking his fingers in a gesture for me to give him my hand. I do, and he lifts me from the floor onto legs as wobbly as a newborn foal.

When I find my feet, I take in the rest of him. Black sort of canvas button-up shirt, open at the neck, showing enough of what's underneath for me to appreciate he's clearly a man that works for a living. His hand is rough, just like his low growl.

I strain to look up, taking in his face and the dark, wavy hair left to fall as it chooses. His clean-shaven angular jaw and unwavering gaze have my nipples perking up as dull contractions tighten my center.

"Your *sister?*" Baldy grunts, narrowing his eyes as I offer a silent shrug and a smile, because I'm not sure what exactly is going on here, but I do know I want more of it.

"My brother is very protective." I glance at the enormous stranger, playing into whatever game this is and realize his eyes are a dark jade green, such a vivid jewel tone that it looks out of place with the rest of him. "Thanks, bro," I manage, delivering a playful punch into his shoulder.

My knuckles are met with rock hard muscle. My throat and mouth turn to a desert while my palms turn clammy.

His eyes leave mine, centering on Baldy as he points toward the floor. "Pick up the rest of her stuff. You made the mess, you clean it up."

He releases my hand, tapping two long, thick fingers onto the wet table-top, nailing the now confused-looking local with a glare that has him bending without a word, picking up my keys, a hairbrush and a bottle of hand sanitizer.

Then my unexpected brother turns his attention back to me, and my nipples give him a sharp salute.

"Pack it up, sis. It's time to go."

He dominates the space like a century old oak, with a sturdy voice to match.

In silent irritation, baldy tosses my belongings onto the table, leaving with a final muttered grumble, stumbling as he turns, trying to gather what's left of his pride as he saunters back toward the bar, yelling for another beer.

Heat and wetness invade the seam of my shorts as my 'brother's' gaze shifts, and, to my horror, I realize I'm still pinching the three pack of Trojans between my fingers. The alcohol is making everything warm and fuzzy as the flush from my face creeps down my chest.

"You have a big night planned?" He cocks a brow as my face flames.

"No, I mean, I've never...this is just..." I stutter. "These aren't for *me*, I don't *wear* them."

Please, mouth, stop.

Tequila and whipped cream shots did this to me.

I shake my head, mumbling unintelligibly to myself as he stares down in silence, his fingers balling and releasing.

"Got it. I'm pretty sure you couldn't hide anything from me in those." He gestures with a nod toward my shorts, and I glance down, tugging at the outside seem in an attempt to lessen the way they are creating a definitive indent between my pussy lips. As I fuss with my shorts, his exotic eyes take a slow walk down my legs to my boots, then back up again, lingering for a beat on my chest as he shakes his head.

He snatches the condoms I forgot I was holding from my hand, flinging them toward a trash can against the wall where they obediently fall into the pile of red solo cups and empty pizza boxes.

The way he looks at me has me rocking back on the heels of my boots, that newborn foal feeling taking hold again.

"Let's go before I have to hurt someone."

"Hurt someone?"

His forearms flex, and wetness floods my lower forty making me rethink the opportunity that has just presented itself.

"Yeah, you may not *be* my sister, but I'd take on this whole bar for you, Daisy."

Daisy?

Lust billows through me, and never in my twenty-one years have I had this sort of reaction to a man. Nothing I felt with Greg even came close. I spent four years with him, and even with all the dry humping he seemed to enjoy so much while keeping his eyes on some live Twitch feed, I never came close to what this tall, dark and erect stranger is making me feel. My heart, my head and my tingling girl parts are awake all together for the first time, and reckless ideas start ping ponging around inside my alcohol addled brain.

"What's your name?" I manage, swallowing the gathering saliva under my tongue, shooting Dolly a look over my shoulder to find her looking like the cream in the middle of a hoedown cookie, with a new sexy guy rocking her on his thigh and an equally sexy brunette rubbing her tits on her back while nuzzling her neck.

"Big brother," he answers in a hoarse grunt, as Dolly catches my eye, giving me a double thumbs up, then an A-ok sign, which means, I'll talk to you later.

"So, okay, *big brother*... No real names? Works for me," I say, pausing a beat to think through what I'm about to say, then finally decide it's time to take the bull by the horns. "How about you buy me one more drink?"

Chapter Two

Price

This dimpled little cowgirl princess with shimmering dark hair the color of my morning black coffee wants me to buy her another drink.

I should say no.

But I don't. Instead, I'm offering her a deal.

"On one condition," I say, pausing on an inhale, trying to clear my head of all the filthy things I want to do to her mouth.

"What condition?" She smirks, puckering those bee-stung lips as she sways a little back and forth.

Don't do it, Price. Walk away.

But I want her out of here, where only my eyes are

on her. Conflict beats inside of me as I clench my jaw, the words stuck in my tight throat. My cock is hard as a lead pipe, as I imagine the impossible. Her. Me. Naked under a waterfall, washing her off after raw-dogging her on her knees in the dirt until she lost consciousness.

Words aren't my friend in the normal course of things, but with her standing there staring up at me? I've flatlined.

My silence seems to defeat her. Her eyes drop, head turning back toward the dance floor.

"Never mind," she mumbles, as the playful twinkle drains from her eyes, and it's like a knife in my heart.

She spins on her toe to walk away, but instinct kicks in. I reach out and catch her wrist, feeling the tiny tick, tick of her pulse against the tips of my fingers.

Her rich brown eyes sparkle as they lift to mine, lashes fluttering, once, twice... She's wearing glittering pink and gold eyeshadow framed by long lashes, and I'm getting lost in her eyes already.

She tilts her head, raising her eyebrows. "Were you going to say something?"

"One more drink," I finally blurt out, holding up a single finger, "but then I get to take you home." Her jaw drops, a smile taking over, but as much as I would kill to *take her home*, I clarify, "I mean, I get to make sure you get home safe."

The smile doesn't fade as she crinkles her nose. "I pick the drink, and you have to promise *me* something."

"Name it," I tell her before I can stop myself.

"After you take me home, there's something I want you to do for me."

Light dances in her warm eyes, heat returning to her cheeks. My heart taps at my ribs as she wrings her canvas purse in a death grip.

She rolls her lips together, red heat spreading over her cheeks as she glances around before pinching an eye shut like she's telling me a deep secret. "Let's just say, I hope you like cherries."

Fuck. Me.

Static crackles over my skin, and I reach down, sliding my hand around the curve of her back. She squeaks as I pull those million-dollar tits tight against my chest. The movement is rough and her eyes round, but she starts teething her lower lip again, eyes locked on mine.

Just remember, don't fall in love. That's off limits.

Off. Off limits.

The only woman in my life is Hailey. There's no room for anyone else. Not for at least the next twelve years.

But when she tosses her bag on the bar top, slipping her warm little hands slip upward, clinging to the back of my neck, joy filling her face, something inside my chest twitches.

"Ripe. Fresh. Sweet cherries," she teases like a brat, and whatever defenses I had crumble.

I've never been good with limits. In fact, pushing them is where I excel.

Especially when it's dangerous.

Chapter Three

Price

This can't be happening to me. Not right now.
Apart from one drunken night I wouldn't remember if not for a pretty fucking undeniable piece of evidence, women and I don't mix. They don't like me, and that's fine because I don't know the first fucking thing about what makes them tick.

But it's not just women that are the problem, it's human beings in general. I don't understand them. I don't get along with them. I don't get this need to connect all the time, to constantly seek approval from the rest of the world.

That might seem odd, coming from someone with a YouTube channel that generates a multi-six-figure income, but that was a pure fucking accident. I've got something people crave. Living vicariously through someone else.

They want to watch someone else doing the dangerous things.

And they love when I fail. When I smack my face into a rock wall or fall on my ass in the mud.

Give me a rope and a challenge, I know what to do, but put me in a social setting of any kind, I'm a fucking duck on skates.

But this *is* happening. It's not a dream.

How do I know?

One, my dick is pressing against the zipper of my pants so hard I'm going to have a permanent impression of the metal teeth along my shaft.

Two, this girl has a smile that could melt the polar ice caps, and I can't help the feeling that I need to make that smile part of my life.

And three, her round face and that left dimple are life changing. I want to start at her lips and lick my way down to what has to be the pussy to end all pussies.

What the hell is happening to me?

When I walked into Earl's, my intention was to blow off some steam. Have a couple beers—alone—and settle into the idea that my high adventure days are over. I'm now the director of an adventure camp in the western upper peninsula of Michigan, raising my daughter as a single father.

I haven't had a night away from Hailey in six

months. As much as every minute with her is better than any minute I lived before her, she's a handful.

Yesterday, she plugged the toilet in our cabin with pinecones, telling me she was doing an experiment on the density of the different varieties and wanted to see which one would sink first.

She's six, for fuck sake. How I'm ever going to live through puberty with her I'm not sure. But one day at a time.

She's with my best friend Ted tonight, who got me in on the camp partnership and has known Hailey since those first days when her mom, Lainy, dropped the bomb on me that my one-night stand made me a father. She took her fucking time telling me, three years fucking years I missed out on, and if she hadn't been battling cancer, I may have never known I had a daughter.

So, my plate is more than full, and I wasn't looking for a hook-up tonight. More people in my life is not what this guy needs. Especially women.

My own fist has served me well all these years, and I don't see any reason to change that. It doesn't talk back or expect conversation or after glow.

But then I saw her sitting on that bar stool, looking like a fucking Daisy Duke wet dream, throwing back shots with a guy who didn't deserve to be in the same state as a perfect ten like her. She's boner-inducing dynamite in a petite curvy package that has my balls ready to unload right here.

Now, she's talking about cherries. And that she's never used a condom. Fuck.

I'm in deep, but even with my hard-on trying to take over my brain, I know this can't happen. Not now.

"What can I get you?" The bartender braces his arms on the counter, looking from me to the dimpled temptation standing barely to my chest.

"I'll have another one of those whipped cream shots." She leans over the bar, her tits resting on top, spilling out from where her shirt is open.

"You mean a blowjob?" he says with a smirk, his eyes locking on her cleavage. My instinct is to rip him from behind the bar and stomp on his head until his brains drain out his ears for looking at her like he'd be winning the lottery if she was on her knees in front of him.

Never gonna happen, bub.

I shift forward, resting my hand on her shoulder as she looks up at me, her cheeks all flushed and those mesmerizing brown doe eyes just asking for trouble.

She's oblivious to the bartender's lecherous look as she yells over the sound of the country music and the growing crowd. "Make that two blowjobs." She holds up her fingers in a 'V' shape, crinkling her nose with an impish bite of her full bottom lip, and I'm gone.

On a hard exhale, I nod to the bartender, reaching into my pocket and pulling out a twenty, slapping it down on the counter and fighting off the invasive pounding thoughts of how tight her pussy must be.

She's swaying a little already. I'm going to let her have this one last shot, but after that, she's cut off. From the time I sat down, I counted her drinks. She threw back four shots while I watched and who knows how many before I got here.

I'll be her bodyguard until I get her home safely, whether she likes it or not, but too much is too much, and the idea of her hurt in any way makes me unreasonably angry. I swear, if she fell down and skinned her fucking knee, I'd take a jackhammer to the sidewalk and destroy it for hurting her.

The bartender slides the two whipped cream topped shots on the bar top, and I roll my eyes. He scoops up the twenty as I wave him off in a keep the change and get the fuck away motion. As I look down, the thought that this delightful curvy angel might not be old enough to drink sinks in.

"They card you when you came in here?" I growl, unsure why I care if she's underage. Unless, of course, she's *under*-under age. Because that would make me a depraved asshole and a possible felon if my control snaps, which, right now, is quite possible.

My mating instinct doesn't seem to care about her age, but I remind myself it doesn't matter. I'm not touching her.

"I'm twenty-one, big brother. Don't worry, I'm legal. *Barely*." She adds a wink and my cock practically comes through my zipper. "Bottoms up."

She raises one of the shots toward my face, but even with her arm fully extended, her hand barely reaches my chin. I fill my lungs until they hurt as I accept the ridiculous drink, unsure how I'm ever going to live without seeing her again.

Her scent cuts through the smell of beer and greasy bar food like a sweet, dark Michigan cherry.

Cherry. That word seems to keep coming up, and it's not helping.

Watching her lick the whipped cream from the top of the shot glass is fucking life changing. I scoop the whipped cream off the top of the shot and throw it to the floor, then bring it to my lips and swallow the sticky sweet liquid then slamming the glass on the counter as she tips hers to her for a tentative sip keeping her glazed eyes pinned to my face.

She lowers the glass an inch, a touch of the leftover white cream decorating her upper and lower lips, and all I want to do is replace it with my own warm, white cream.

"This is my third blowjob tonight," she whispers with another wink and a deep breath, which makes her tits rise in the tight, tied up cowgirl plaid shirt, delivering another sledgehammer blow to my resolve.

I reach down and manhandle my dick, trying to find a less painful position for the swollen motherfucker as she downs the cream-covered liquor, and I swear, I already want to marry this girl.

But I can't. I promised myself when Hailey's mother passed away, and I took on full custody, I wouldn't let a woman divide my attention. No evil stepmothers for my little girl. When it comes to her, I will never compromise.

She will have the upbringing I wish I had.

Being a single dad has been the best and most challenging part of my life, but I'm all in. I knew from the moment we met when she was three, I was going to dedicate the rest of my life to her.

Her mother, who I only vaguely remembered, offered to do a paternity test, but I didn't need it. I knew in my heart that Hailey was mine. She has my green eyes and the same crooked smile as my little brother.

She is my number one, forever. First priority, no matter what my dick might be trying to convince me otherwise right now.

Even so, I glare at all the men watching Daisy, letting them know she's off limits. Just because I won't be deflowering her, doesn't mean I'm going to let some other fucker have that privilege.

I reach down and run the pad of my thumb over her top lip, swiping away some left-over cream, then bring it to my mouth to suck it off. The first moment I saw her sitting on that bar stool, I was captivated. Her soft body would feel perfect under me. Diving face first between her legs would turn me inside out.

My heart ticks away in some crazy Morse code, but I push away the message it's trying to send.

She blinks, her chest heaving, cheeks flushed. She's a fucking knockout, and even if I was in the market, I know she's out of my league. Besides the age difference of twelve years, I've never been known for my looks. I'm thick, solid and sure, if you took my picture from the neck down, I might understand how someone would find the body somewhat attractive, but my face is another matter.

Being into extreme sports since my teen years, and later into extreme wilderness excursions, I've broken my nose three times, dislocated my jaw once and cracked my eye socket when my carabiner snapped as I climbed the sheer face of a mountain in South America, five hundred miles from the nearest hospital.

I straightened it myself the best I could, and it healed like you'd think.

"So, big brother." She smiles and that tightness in my chest turns into a sharp pain. God, I want her to call me that when I'm ten inches deep in her hot little baby maker. "Ready to make sure your little sister gets home safe and sound?"

My temples start to pound. She's playing with me. I get it, and I'm here for it. But, on the other hand, I know I'm getting myself into something I shouldn't.

Besides my daughter, my only focus right now is my new position as director of Camp WanderLust. It will be my other baby for the next couple years, trying to turn it into a reality show worthy wilderness experience.

I've made a name for myself on YouTube, and

although my social media celebrity has its downside, it's allowed my bank account to flourish. When Hailey's mom's illness turned south, and I realized parenting was going to become full-time, it was a no-brainer to pivot to a life designed for more stability while still keeping my feet in the wild world that I love.

The only woman in my life would be my daughter.

"This way." I reach for my little Daisy Duke fairy, loving the way she twines her delicate fingers between my knotty, calloused ones. I scoop up her bag, and lead the way.

I won't deny I'm as happy as a pig in shit to get her out of here before I have to lay out one of the locals for eye fucking her in those barely-there shorts and tied-up shirt.

She toddles behind me, scuffing her cowboy boots with every unsteady step, until I weave us through the crowd and out the door into the cool night air.

The change of atmosphere gives me a momentary reset, grateful for a cleansing breath and a look at the dark, star-filled sky.

Outside, her cherry scent mixes with the smell of the pine forest that blankets the top of the Michigan border, and I know I'd give my left nut to get a lick of her.

She squeezes my fingers and I feel it down into my balls.

"Look," she says, her manner turning serious, although it's hard to take anything she says right now as gospel. From the thickness of her words and the sway in her steps, she's clearly under the influence.

She scratches at her neck, then fiddles with the gold four leaf clover pendant around her neck, zipping it back and forth on the chain a few times as we walk through the parking lot toward the street.

"I'm staying at the Black Swan bed and breakfast, just over there." She points an unsteady finger across the street, but I saw the place she's talking about when I drove through town last week. It's across the park, down about a block certainly within walking distance but there's no fucking way I'm letting her walk there without me.

"Got it." I want to ask her why she and her friend are in town, because no way they're local, but knowing more about her is only going to make it harder to leave her there and walk away. "I'll make sure you get home safe, just like I said."

God, I wonder if she's wet.

Stop thinking about her fucking pussy dipshit. You're walking her back, that's it.

"I want to ask you something...*brother*." She blinks up at me as I slow my steps, my strides three times the length of hers.

Just thinking of walking her to the bed and breakfast has heat charging up the back of my neck. The way her thighs are rubbing together as we walk is fucking distracting, and I steal a long, depraved look at the way her round ass is working the back of those shorts, the curved bottoms of her cheeks hanging out, making it hard to breathe.

"Ask away," I grumble, unsure what her question is going to be but already knowing it's going to be trouble.

"See, I like that we aren't going to share our names. You're just big brother, and I'm little sister. That works out perfect because, see, I want to lose my virginity."

Full fucking stop.

I look around to make sure there's no cameras because this can't be real.

But, she keeps talking and I'm all fucking ears. "So, I want to do it, and I don't want any strings. I feel like you're the guy." The words are thick as molasses as she looks up at me, and fucking angels start singing.

She wants me to pop her cherry and never see her again?

That's the most impossible thing I've ever heard of.

My resolve is fraying like a rope over a sharp cliff.

"You've been doing shots all night. You're not thinking straight. What have you had to eat today?"

The words taste like arsenic in my mouth. All my tongue wants to do is say 'yes, I'll introduce your untouched sacred ground there to every inch of my dick while planting myself in your belly so you'll be mine forever'.

All my brain wants is to put her over my knee and teach her never to proposition a near stranger in the middle of a dark street after doing shots all night.

I'd turn that ripe, round apple ass of hers red as

punishment, then let her know the new order of her life. I'd kiss away her tears and explain I'll forever only want what's best for her. Keeping her safe would be my number one priority.

But that's not happening, Price.

Not. Gonna. Happen.

Chapter Four

Price

It's nothing new to me that my decision-making skills leave a lot to be desired.

Right now is one of those moments, because I'm following Daisy through the foyer of The Black Swan bed and breakfast instead of leaving her at the door and walking away.

A quick goodnight, nice to meet you, glad you're safe...any of these would have worked. Then I could have turned and left, knowing the little bundle of hotness was safely back in her room, destined to be the fuel for an angry beat-off session in the shower back at camp.

Instead, my eyes are digging into the soft flesh of her

lower ass cheeks hanging out the back of her shorts as she turns her face over her shoulder, holding a finger to her lips in a '*shhhhh*' gesture, then points to a door at the top of the stairs.

"Follow me. My room is right there."

Fuck me. My boots make clunking sounds on the wooden stairs, no matter how softly I try to step.

Daisy digs in her bag, retrieving a single key attached by a silver ring to a small, stuffed black swan, and aims it unsteadily at the door knob.

"Jussa sec." Her balance seems to be deteriorating with each step. I knew I shouldn't have bought her another shot. She gives me another one of her 'shhhh' gestures, only this time she adds a wink, and I already know this girl could ask me for my left nut, and I'd gladly deliver it to her on a silver platter. "The knob keeps moving."

She taps the tip of the key all around its intended target, missing the jagged key slot four times before I can't take it anymore.

"Here." I slip my hand over hers, guiding the key into the slot, pushing it in as my mind takes the moment to think of how my dick would feel sliding into her soft silky warmth.

"You're susha a gennleman," she slurs with a cute little crinkle of her nose.

"You don't know me. I'm no gentleman."

Get your ass out of here before she can invite you in.

The door swings open, sending Daisy falling

forward as her balance gives way. I catch her in the crook of my arm with a grunt, just inches before her face hits the floor. Holding her soft, curvy body against mine sends my balls into spasm.

"Mrs. Kelsey said after ten is quiet time." She holds a finger to her lips, tipping her head twice in an invitation for me to come into her room.

Leave, asshole. You need to leave.

My feet ignore my brain. I set her onto her feet and lead us both, my arm still clutching around the soft skin of her exposed midriff, through the door and into the room.

Inside, it's like a flower shop exploded. Everything that is not made of antique oak is a fury of floral patterns in pinks, lavenders and greens.

Daisy drifts away from my grip, leaving me staring around the ample bedroom, feeling like a two-hundred-and-seventy-pound sore thumb sticking out in this feminine space.

"You wanna drink?" She spins on her boot toward a bottle of Chardonnay that sits corked on the top of a small round table against the wall. She drops her bag on the floor next to the bed as she takes a few swaying steps toward the wine. "It *came* witha room."

"No. And you don't either," I growl as she turns, staring at my mouth.

I sidestep, reaching out to snatch the bottle away, setting it on the floor by the closet door.

"But—" She looks like I took away her favorite toy,

but she's had enough. I can't shake the low burning anger in my gut that she's let a stranger into her room with her half in the bag.

What if that bald asshole had walked her back? Or any of the myriad lecherous locals that had their eye on her back in the bar?

"No buts." I turn in a slow circle, spotting a six-pack of bottled water on the floor next to an open suitcase. "This is what you can drink."

I step that way, taking a moment to memorize her scent, the way she makes me feel, all of it. I want to remember all of these moments, because I know this can't go anywhere, and for the rest of my life I'll be wishing things could have been different.

What's one night? One last sendoff...

I crack open the twist-off cap, battling my urges and my conflicted conscience, then hold it to those puckered pink lips. "Drink. You need to hydrate."

She keeps her lips shut for a beat, but I stand steady, nodding at her to comply, and with a roll of her eyes she draws a swig of the water into her mouth.

"One more," I say as she blinks, giving me that doe-eyed look that could get her anything she asked for if she really tried.

I hold the bottle up, letting her take a long drink until I'm somewhat satisfied she's got something other than alcohol in her stomach, then set it on the table next to her bag.

God, she's fucking gorgeous, standing there with a

single drip of the water traversing down her chin. I already know walking out that door is going to be painful. How will I function, knowing she's out in the world without me?

Seeing other men. Fucking other men.

Christ, no, I don't want to even imagine that. I'll choose to believe she's a fucking nun before I think of her in someone else's arms.

That first moment I touched her, emotion surged through me, the same intensity as the first time I saw my daughter.

Those deep brown eyes watch me, and even through the alcohol I can see she's no bimbo. The Daisy Duke stripper outfit aside, this girl is smart and alive. What's a girl like her doing in Ompotomic, Michigan?

My mouth waters as she toes each of her boots off the opposite foot, then picks them up and sets them neatly next to her open suitcase.

"Isn't this room great?" she asks, running her finger over a palm-sized, blooming pink rose on the wall.

I draw a breath through my teeth, taking note of her smile, watching her finger trace the petals of the wallpaper rose, imagining it tracing my lips, dancing down my neck, my chest, ending at the straining button of my pants, popping it open, then working the zipper down...

Lost in my progressing fantasy, I realize I didn't answer her question.

"You're in it, so yeah, it's great." That's the truth, and

from the way she's biting into her bottom lip, something I said is working for her.

"You look a little out of place." She steps my way. In her bare feet she's a couple inches shorter than in the bar and our size difference is almost ridiculous.

My pulse hammers as I tell myself to step back and ball it out that door, but my feet are stuck rock solid on the pink and green rose-patterned rug.

I curse my moral compass, because all I want to do is drag this precious morsel over to that floral nightmare of a bed, rip off those shorts, and destroy that tart cherry like a wrecking ball.

I'd nut in three strokes, I'm sure. I'd fill her like a fucking bull.

"There's a bed," she chirps, with a little teasing sashay of her hips, and sweat trickles down my spine. Our proximity to a bed has my windpipe clogging with all the filthy things I want to say to her.

"Yeah, you should get in it," I grumble, already knowing my heart has signed on the dotted line with this girl and the memory of her will haunt me to my grave.

"I should, you're right. You should lay down with me. My *big brother* could tell me a story while I fall asleep." She slides her hand down the flat of her chest, jiggling back and forth, and I can't tell if it's the booze or her just being a tease.

I bet it's both.

"I should go," I hear myself say as her eyes start to flutter, her head swings around on her neck like a bobblehead, knees buckling. Jesus, she's passing out. I lunge forward my hand slipping around her middle as I groan and my eyes devour her fertile body before she hits the floor.

Panic sweeps through me. Once again, that thought that someone else could have come back here with her assaults me like a bullet to the chest.

Pulling her against me, her limbs are limp in my arms, her lips parted as fear ices my veins. "*Daisy,*" I hiss, realizing I don't know her name.

I tell myself she's just had too much to drink. She'll sleep it off and wake up thirsty and craving a greasy burger, but seeing her in my arms, helpless and unconscious, has me as unsteady as I was that time Hailey dove into the swimming pool at her mother's house and sank to the bottom.

This morsel of a girl is going to rip my heart out. That, I already know, and something else I know is I'd gladly let her, if it wasn't for the promises I made to myself and my daughter.

"*Daisy,*" I say with more vigor this time, lowering her onto the bed on her side, tilting her head so that if that alcohol decides to turn her stomach inside out, she won't choke.

I brush the backs of my fingers across her forehead, pushing a silky strand of that rich, coffee-colored hair behind her ear, cursing myself for buying her another drink.

God, I could take her right now. If I was a worse

man, I'd strip her down to her birthday suit, spread her thick thighs and do as I please.

My fingers trail down. Over her temple, her jaw, traversing the side of her neck until I follow her collar bone to where her sternum begins.

Just a little lower and the billowing flesh of her breasts could be in my hand. God, I shouldn't be here. I should have left her at the door. Or I could just beat off while she sleeps, leaving a surprise all over her tits and face to remember me by.

Jesus, the thought has me ready to nut right here.

A blip of anger smolders inside me. This isn't fair. Meeting this girl, now, when my life is off limits to a relationship. What would have happened if she hadn't passed out, and things...happened?

She'd expect more from me? Be a boyfriend and a good man? Fucking understand the nuances of a romantic relationship? I'm not even the drunk one, but I'm spinning and intoxicated. Confused and—

A smile crests her pink lips as her eyes flutter open, hazy but focused on me, and she says, "Guess you're a gentleman after all. You could have done whatever you wanted with me...passed out."

Jesus. This girl.

"You're faking?" I grimace. She's testing me for sure. "Don't ever do that again, or I'll turn you over and ripen that ass of yours."

Her playful eyes turn shy and sad as she tugs a shoulder upward. "Yes, Sir. Big brothers are mean."

Those words render me helpless and speechless.

Yes, Sir.

Big brother.

What the fuck is next? The tightness in my chest increases. I want to protect her with every inch of my being. Having her soft body against me, all the reasons this can't happen blow away like ashes in the wind.

Lying next to me, she seems even smaller than before, but everywhere our bodies touch feels right.

Again, I mentally list all the reasons this can't happen, but now, they don't seem to matter.

If I walked away, I'd destroy this place on my way out. Flipping over all the little lace-covered tables and bloodying my knuckles on every mirror as I punched them, hating the sight of my own face.

As if she's reading my mind, her hand comes to rest on my cheek. There's a tightness in her face like she wants to smile, but something is holding it back.

"Just—" I grimace toward the ceiling, gathering the strength and courage to tell her I have to leave, but the trust in her eyes is throwing me for a loop. Her opulent tits are now spilling out of the top of her shirt. The snap that was holding them in must have popped when I caught her from fake-falling, and all I can think about is shoving my dick between those soft mounds, her mouth wide, tongue out as I buck my hips, straddling her body, delivering a creamy white shower all over her fucking face.

When her hand drifts south, fingers walking down

my chest, over my clenched abs to stop on my belt buckle, I'm frozen in time.

"Are you faking, too?" she whisper-hisses, rubbing her knuckles down the obvious length of my arousal, and I'm one second from erupting in my pants.

I bolt up off the bed, the loss of her touch and her softness next to me sending me into a wave of dark grief, but there's no way this can happen. It's not just my no-women-until-my-daughter-is-grown-up vow, or my focus on the camp, but, Jesus, she's half in the bag. I might not understand people, but I know the difference between right and wrong. No way I'm fucking a girl without her being present.

Correction, dick, no way you're fucking any girl.

Confusion and the pain in my balls has me barreling toward the door I assume leads to the bathroom.

Inside, I don't bother with the light, slamming the hard oak door behind me and falling against the nearest wall. My brains have gone offline, because within a second I've got my belt unbuckled, zipper down, rage fucking my fist, begging for a shred of relief so I can think straight and leave this perfect girl untouched.

But even in my lust blindness, I realize the space is stuffy and small, my breathing muffled.

I'm not in the bathroom. I'm in the fucking closet.

My engorged dick doesn't care, my breathing is ragged as the vision of tit-fucking her on that nightmare of a comforter that looks like a flower shop threw up everywhere taunts me from behind my closed lids.

"Fuck!" I grunt, as I get my shaft in my hand and squeeze.

Even in my madness, I won't touch her, no matter how tempting the offer. She's drunk. Drunk enough that even with consent, it wouldn't count.

So I'm leaning against the wall in a fucking closet, with my johnson in my hand, the taste of that god awful blow job shot like vomit in my mouth.

A soft knock on the door is followed immediately by the knob turning. In my haste, I didn't bother with the small detail of seeing if the door had a lock.

"Are you okay?" Daisy's concern is the calm to my bellowing storm, as my hand rifles back and forth on my shaft, desperate for a shred of relief.

"Fine. Just..." Another five strokes, faster, faster. "I need...a...minute." I grimace against the impending orgasm, my hand moving in a fury in the darkness, her face taunting me in my imagination.

I grab at the knob. Just another stroke, two, and I'll be done. Just keep the door closed a few more seconds---

The metal knob pulls off into my hand, the door swings open, a slice of light cutting across my face and down my body, illuminating the source of my madness.

Daisy's cheeks ripen again, eyes wide as I thrust into my jacking grip, dropping the brass knob to the floor with a clunk.

Her hands fly to cover her open mouth, but I can't stop.

I'm not available for what I see in her eyes. I'm not

available, period. I had to do something to convince her of that fact. I need her to see me for what I am. A man without fucking availability. A man that has nothing to offer a girl like her.

My heart is already involved, and that's more dangerous than any mountain I've climbed or wilderness I've conquered. She would expect attention, a home, time, a reasonable man, and she deserves to be the center of someone's world, but I already orbit around Hailey. My bandwidth for anything else is nonexistent.

"You like what you do to me?" I say, the words taking on a harder edge.

"I'm sorry?" she says breathlessly, and I notice she's now barefooted. Her toenails are painted in various shades of pink and red, like the petals of the flowers all over the walls that surround her.

"I'm not the kind of man you need, Daisy."

"How do you know what I need?" Her hands brush the crease of her cleavage, the tips of her fingers toying with the fabric where the snap is barely keeping the shirt from exposing her swelling breasts.

The charge of lust in her eyes tells me what she's about to do before it happens, and I'm helpless to stop it.

Her fingers work the knot holding up the plaid shirt just under her breasts, then she works the snaps open as my hand moves in a blur, taking in the perfection in front of me. She's wearing a lace-trimmed cotton bra slash tank top, which she pushes down under her breasts, letting them fall free over the fabric, and they are even better than I could have imagined.

Desire and anger merge inside of me again, as I imagine her coming here with someone else. Someone that would take everything she's offering and probably more.

"You shouldn't have let me come up here with you," I say hoarsely, reaching out and taking a fist of her hair. "It's dangerous. I won't touch you. I just need...relief."

To my shock, she's fallen to her knees, tongue tracing on her lips. "You don't have to touch me. But I can touch you."

God, how do I teach her a lesson without giving in to my urges? I want her to kick me out, push me away. Why can't she see me for what I am? Unavailable, broken and way below her paygrade.

"You know what men do to drunk girls that invite them back to their room?" I demand, my hand slowing, letting her see the monstrosity of what she's done.

"No. I've never invited a man back to my room. Drunk or not. I've never done much of ...anything." She glides her tongue along her bottom lip, looking up at my dick as her hands press on the tension of my thighs.

"I'm going to teach you then." Pain shoots behind my eyes and I snap. "Open your mouth, and I'm going to show you."

"I'm ready for my lesson—"

I snuff out whatever else she was going to say with my dick between her lips. How much can a man take?

"That's what men think about when you're around. All those guys in the bar, this is what they were imagining while they were buying you shots." My words are muffled in the enclosed closet. Folded sheets and blankets are piled on shelves, empty metal hangers rattling as I cling to the bar, my knees trembling with the warmth of her welcoming mouth.

I release her hair, my hand slipping around the granite-hard length, and I start to pump the skin up and down as her lips pop around the ridge of the head, encasing me in wet warmth.

"Jesus." My eyes roll back as I bite the inside of my cheek, fighting off the orgasm that is already inching up from my balls, ready to empty before I get a single pump down her pretty throat.

I jack off as she pulls away and I watch in horror and awe as she makes a throaty sound, then drops a blob of spit on the swollen head, smiling like she just won the biggest stuffed animal at the country fair.

"I saw some Tiktok where the girl said 'you gotta spit on that thang'."

I'm speechless, which is nothing really new, as she starts to take me in and out, working her way down, her lips stretched around the girth as a low, pleased moan vibrates through me.

"Play with your tits," I order, barely remembering my own name by this point. My voice is hoarse as I watch her obey, hands cupping the weight of them, eyes locking with mine. No fear, but more understanding than I deserve right now.

Her mouth is magic, working faster, wetter, as I move my hand from my dick to the side of her head, fisting her hair once again, showing her the pace I need. I'm as drunk as she is, my vision wavering as knots gather in my belly.

If this girl has never done this, no one told her mouth.

I watch as she pinches her nipples, rolling them, moaning as the pleasure I was chasing becomes a mutual goal.

She gags and coughs, tears streaming down her blushed cheeks as I push harder, deeper, harder, deeper, thinking I'm pushing her away with my rough demands, but instead, she's whimpering, kneading her soft flesh, her distended nipples tight as she works them between her fingers.

My hips jerk forward as I exert full control over her head, her hair twined between my thick fingers as I feel her throat open to me, and she delivers the final death blow.

She drops one hand from her breast, spreading her knees on the wood floor, grabbing between her legs as her hips start to rock.

I bite back the roar that gathers in my throat as her eyes tell me she would give me her all right now, if only I'd take it.

My orgasm breaks free, as I choke and bellow in

broken, inhuman sounds. Hot spurts of cum race from my balls, bursting down her throat as I drive myself deeper than she should be able to take. My orgasm locks its jaws around my protests, taking on a life of its own, betraying me with its power and intensity.

I'm not just coming, I'm delivering part of me into her. Part of me I swore I wouldn't share.

I come and come until I'm shaking, sweat dripping down the crease of my back, my breathing ragged and unsteady.

I draw my spent dick from her gaping mouth, her hands frozen in place. Fingers dig into the soft flesh of her tit, her others gripping between the apex of her thighs. She's so fucking beautiful, it makes me choke.

I hate myself for giving in and putting her here, in front of a man that can't give himself to her the way her eyes tell me she would do for me.

I battle away the urge to walk, to leave her there on her knees with my cum in her belly. Instead, I tuck my erection back into my pants, smart enough to realize I don't have the right words for this moment.

"Brother," she sighs, and that word hits me like a locomotive. "Or, do you prefer Daddy? You seem like you'd be a great daddy."

Did she just say what I think she said?

Holy shit. Did that word just carve out a place in my heart for her forever?

"Daisy." I reach down, taking her hands in mine, lifting her from her knees, tits swaying with each step as

I walk her toward the bed. "Time for sleep," I grunt, the words sticking in my throat as the confusion and disappointment in her eyes becomes my shackle of guilt.

I fling the bedding back, hoping I can last one more minute, one more test, as she slips between the flowered sheets. "Lay with me...Daddy." Her whisper is a soft order I can't refuse. "I don't want to be alone."

How this girl is ever alone, I can't puzzle through. "My clothes stay on, but I'll stay," I say as the alarm bells and sirens scream in my head.

I cover her, tucking the bedding around her making sure there's another layer between us, then lower my massive body onto the bed, listening to the frame and the springs struggle under my weight.

I'm thankful that we both seem to realize talking isn't what either of us needs right now. Jesus, how I want to give her what she gave me, but I'm already so far over the line, I may never find my way back. If I taste that sweet pussy, it will break me.

Her light breathing turns heavy, as I stare at the stained glass light fixture over the bed replaying every second since the moment I walked into Earl's and set my eyes on her.

I lie like that until I lose feeling in my hand and I really need to piss. As much as I am enjoying being in bed with her, nature calls.

I ease my arm out, allowing myself this one last night of indulgence before I go back to camp, back to my new life, leaving the memory of this night and the girl in the bar I only know as Daisy forever.

I take slow, easy steps toward the bathroom door. As I walk by her suitcase, I see it.

There, folded in the clothes of her open suitcase, is a lime green t-shirt. Nobody would *choose* that shade of green. I know nothing about fashion, but I know that. I told Ted when I took the job as Camp WanderLust director that I'm not wearing one, and he reluctantly agreed, knowing when I say I'm not doing something, I'm not fucking doing it.

I reach down, tugging it out from the other clothes and turn it over, and sure enough, there on the front is the camp insignia. With a name printed above.

Summer Greer. Counselor, Summer 2024.

Fuck.

Chapter Five

Summer

I bury my head in the pillow, hazy details of last night trying to break through the pounding hangover fog.
I remember big boots.
Big brother?
Green eyes. Beautiful green eyes.
And a face that's taken some hard hits but is somehow in its own way…beautiful.
I wanted to kiss him. I wanted him to kiss me. I smile remembering him telling me to drink water, that I'd had enough alcohol. Bossy. A bossy, strong, safe man and —good God.
There were blow job shots.

Then, a blow job and I don't even know his name.

I try to open my eyes, but the world is a horrible mix brightness, discomfort and disbelief.

"Ow, my head," I complain, flattening a hand over my face in an attempt to block out the sun that's decided to be up so damned early...

Early.

"Shit. Shit, *shit, SHIT.*" I throw off the comforter, as I turn to see the red glowing numbers of the digital clock on the bedside table. "*Shit!*"

Kicking away the sheet that's wrapped itself around my feet, I half fall out of bed. The floor feels like it's moving under my feet, throwing me off balance. My clothes from last night are scattered like confetti, and with no time to find clean ones I scramble for anything within reach.

Where the hell is my shirt?

As I frantically search, I spot the note, folded neatly so that it stands like a tent on the dresser. *Little Sister*, is written in black ink, in rough, thick letters.

He could have done *anything* to me. I wonder if he did... And if he did, whether I'd mind. Maybe, but only because I want to remember it.

I open the paper, lay it on the table next to my bag, reading as I grab at the closest pair of shorts and shimmy myself into them.

First, I want you to know that I didn't touch you after you passed out.

You didn't make it easy though. You were teasing me even in your sleep.

Your cherry is still 100% intact.

There's a bottle of water here, I want you to drink all of it as soon as you're awake. And I've also left you a carabiner. It might not seem like much, but it almost killed me once, and I don't know... I just always kept it close as a reminder of how quickly things can change. It's all I have to give you, to let you know I think you're special. One of a kind.

Sorry, I have to go. Drink your water.

Your Big Brother

I re-read the note as I secure my bralette and the plaid shirt from last night onto my torso, working the buttons closed, leaving the tails to hang down instead of retying the inappropriate boob-enhancing knot Dolly insisted on last night, and let it fall to cover my belly.

I stuff my feet into socks and my new hiking boots with embroidered flowers on the leather and I know I look ridiculous but there's no time for primping.

I stuff any of my remaining belongings into my pink Vera Bradley suitcase and tug the zipper around the edge, pulling the handle out until it clicks in place.

My heart is aching more than my head. It's ridiculous to imagine that I have some sort of connection to the surly, well-endowed man from last night, right? Still, I trace the curling lines of his handwriting with a fingertip.

Tequila really does make you crazy.

I drink down the water, hopping on one foot as I work my socks and boots on, thankful for the cool water washing away the remnants of my hangover mouth.

I'm heading toward the door with one quick look back at the flower garden of a room where I gave my first blow job, taking one last side step, picking up the chipped green aluminum clip thing from the nightstand, and securing it on the belt loop of my shorts with a melancholy ache in my chest as I head out the door.

It's an unusual gift I suppose, especially for a girl that has no idea really what a carabiner is or does, but somehow it feels personal. Almost intimate, like he left me the most valuable thing he had. A part of him.

Shit. I'm so late...get it together, girl.

My hair is frizzed and half stuck to my face. I stink of booze. And I have no time to do anything about it.

Perfect first impressions.

I find my phone in my bag, which stinks of the spilled beer and whiskey, the screen filled with texts and calls from Dolly.

I read as I fly down the hallway toward the stairs.

Dolly: If I don't hear from you, or you don't get here by the time orientation is over, I'm calling the ranger to come look for you. Okay, gotta go, the new director of the camp is coming in to do orientation...please be okay. Just hungover and deflowered...

I shoot her a quick, *I'm okay, on my way, cover for me until I get there* text, so she's not losing her mind. Then I hit the staircase, my boots clunking along with my suitcase behind me.

On the bottom step, one of the wheels from my bag snaps. It stays half connected, thank God, but it's making a weird sound and my bag is rolling unevenly behind me as I move through the doorway toward the front desk.

There's an elderly couple checking in with Mrs. Kelsey and they turn my way. As does Mrs. Kelsey herself.

And her glare of disapproval could shame the Pope.

"Um, hi, just checking out," I say, ignoring their judgmental looks. Back straight, eyes open. No walk of shame here, folks. I hold out my key and Mrs. Kelsey takes it gingerly between two pinched fingers as though she's holding a rat by its tail.

"Rough night?"

"Great night, actually." I turn to the man beside me and give him my best smile as his eyes lock onto my chest, then quickly dart away when his wife delivers a hard elbow to his ribs.

Come on...

"I hope you *enjoyed* your stay," Mrs. Kelsey says pointedly, then adds, "I'll be in touch if there are any damages to the room."

I offer an A-okay sign and turn toward the door, dragging my sad, wobbly suitcase behind.

Out in the early morning fresh air and sunshine, I fast walk to my VW Bug, a graduation gift from my parents, pop the trunk tossing my suitcase inside with a thunk, then throw myself behind the wheel and start her up.

With a quick look in the rearview, I see Earl's bar in the distance. My heart clenches as my mouth waters, remembering the other gift the tall, brotherly stranger left me last night.

* * *

There's no one in sight as I walk from the small dirt parking lot near the camp entry, following the sound of a man's voice coming from a log cabin type structure about the size of a small grocery store at the end of a winding gravel path.

"Shit, shit, shit." I hate being late. I'm never late.

It must be the main hall, made of logs with a rough cut stone base, standing out against the backdrop of wood chalets and old-fashioned canvas tents in the distance.

My last reckless summer, which took off like a rocket last night, smells like pine trees and looks like a scene out of Grizzly Adams.

Another show my mother forced me to watch growing up. We were city folks, but she must have had a thing for flannel-wearing men with unruly beards.

I sneak inside, swatting at a single thread from a spider web shining in the morning sun inside the door, heat exploding over my skin as I scan the area for one of the eight-legged monsters lying in wait to attack.

When I ascertain the coast is clear from any arachnids, a flash from last night of how my fake brother's crazy green eyes watched me as I took my first dick in my mouth has that familiar tension gathering in my core.

I tip toe around a corner, settle my suitcase with its squeaky wheel against a log wall as I push open the back door to a large room filled with a sea of folding chairs occupied by bright green shirt wearing camp staff here for orientation.

I scan the group for Dolly as the deep voice coming from the front of the room vibrates down into my bones, and I freeze, turning in a slow circle, my eyes lighting on the speaker in the front of the room.

"Your job is to focus on the campers. Some of the activities are dangerous, their safety is top priority." It's *him*. Oh my God, my brother is standing at the front of the room, addressing the staff like he's the…boss.

I slink forward, wishing I'd packed my invisibility cloak.

"To keep everyone focused, there's a strict no fraternization policy. Anyone caught engaging in…" His eyes fan my way and his gravelly voice catches and stalls when he sees me. For a few heartbeats, it's just me and him again and all the thrill and emotion from last night starts to drown me. Everyone else disappears in a puff of smoke as his eyes feel like they touch me, making me shiver. "Fraternization," he finishes in a distracted mumble.

I might have been drunk, but I wasn't so drunk that I

don't remember what the man who made sure I got back to the B & B safely, who refused to take my cherry, who let me *suck his dick* while I called him my Big Brother, looks like.

"*Summer!*" I hear the hiss of my name. Following the sound, I spot Dolly a few rows ahead from where I'm standing, every eye in the small crowd of lime green t-shirts locked on me in my short shorts and rumpled shirt. "*Here,*" she whispers, pointing to the empty seat beside her, and I turtle into my shoulders as I shuffle her way.

I slink into the cool metal chair as she turns to me. "Where were you?" she whispers.

"I—"

She nods toward the front of the room where my *brother* is still standing silent, as a wave of low mumbling voices courses through the room. "That's *the* guy you left with last night, right?"

My skin flashes as he goes back to his speech about no fraternization.

Pretty sure he fraternized right down my throat last night.

I grab Dolly's wrist jerking it back as she raises a finger to point toward the front of the room. "Do you think I don't know that? Don't point."

"I thought you might not recognize him. You were knee deep in the hoopla last night."

"Did you know he was my new boss?" I lean in, keeping my eyes down on my boots as I squeeze my fingers into my palms.

"What?" Her eyebrows arch. "No! Last year the director was this old woman named Mavis. The year before that it was some creepy-ass dude who kept staring at my tits the whole time. They didn't have a *no fraternization policy* that year, I can tell you."

She screws up her face with a silent gagging expression, as my 'big brother', emphasis on *big*, turns and waves toward a more polished looking man standing off toward the edge of the room.

"This is Mr. Fletcher. He's from the Adventure Channel. They're thinking of turning Camp WanderLust into a reality show, and they're here to observe. There are release forms for everyone to sign because they've installed cameras in the public areas of the camp. He's just here to see whether what we have here might be right for their network."

Big brother ushers the middle-aged man with a receding hairline and an uncomfortable looking brown suit to take over with a wave of his hand.

"Hey there everyone." The guy looks uncomfortable, brushing the bit of hair on the top of his head back with his fingers and from what I can tell, he's a behind the camera sort of guy. "Thanks, Mr. Webber. Everyone knows the famous Price Webber here and your boss's content creation and YouTube fame are why we're here. Now that he's settling down to run the camp, we see an opportunity for more than just a YouTube channel. But, we will see. Just be yourselves and pretend we're not here."

Dolly leans over to whisper, "Your new boyfriend's famous. I hadn't heard of him, but from what some of the other counselors said, he's a big deal in the adrenaline junkie world."

"He's not my boyfriend," I mutter, but inside my head a plan is wiggling itself together.

No fraternization policy or not, I think I've found my Matt Dillon.

Chapter Six

Price

After the team meeting, I practically trample the staff that stand between me and my prize. Anger coils inside me. At myself.

I shouldn't have bolted like I did last night, but when I saw she was going to be on my staff, I fucking panicked like a kid caught with his pants down. I suck with people. Knowing how to handle most normal situations challenges me.

Then, when I tried to casually ask Ted about a counselor named Summer Greer...

He told me she's the girl we hired as the ages six through eight cabin monitor but also...Hailey's speech therapist.

Fuck. I want to be the dad my daughter needs. I want to break the cycle of shitty parenting that goes back three generations in my family.

It's only been a year since we've been together full time, and when I found out kids at her school were teasing her because of her lisp, I damn near burned the place to the ground. After I scared the shit out of the principal and her teacher, they said she might get some help from a speech therapist.

The summer camp and our move was already planned, so when Ted came across a counselor's application that had some speech therapy background on it, I told him to get her here.

Now, here she is, and I'm totally fucked.

All I want is to carry her back to my office, shove her over my desk and mount her like a junkyard dog. I can practically hear the sound of wet flesh slapping, her breath being driven from her lungs with every pump, pump, pump.

And then give her more, because I'll never be able to stop when it comes to her. I'm surprised I'm not getting complaints about the obvious hard-on tenting the front of my combat pants ever since she walked in the room.

I damn near kicked the door down when she disappeared into the ladies' room before I could chase her down.

She emerged wearing her Camp WanderLust t-shirt and our standard khaki shorts, and the fuck if she doesn't make the uniform look like Victoria's Secret on steroids.

She's tamed her hair into two braids tied with little lavender ribbons, as I watch her park her wobbling suitcase next to a bookcase filled with lime green bins with each camper's name on the side.

Taking on the camp with my friend Ted will not be without its challenges for me. But I agreed that sticking with the standing schedule of a youth camp this summer would be a good way to ease into the closest thing to a job I've had in a decade.

As she fists her hips, her make-up freshened and a shimmering pink lipstick applied to the lips that were around my cock, our eyes find each other.

My fingers twitch as I start her way, remembering how her hair felt clutched between them.

A few other staff are gathered around as everyone does the expected mingling after the meeting.

The main hall is used for activities and meals, and I pick up from the group standing around me that the mounted boars' heads and stuffed black bear in the corner might not be PC. I don't care right now.

They're talking, but I'm processing none of it. My eyes are locked on her as she scans the room, looking unsure, her gaze flickering over me with an impish smile, and I walk away from the other counselors without a goodbye.

"About last night," I start, barely able to form words, remembering how I had the hardest orgasm of my life hours ago in her mouth.

"That's a movie isn't it? 'About last night'..." She

clicks her front teeth together, nipping at her manicured fingernail, and Jesus, I want that smile with me for the rest of my life. "Anyway, it's fine. We both knew it was no strings. I was a little..." She tugs her lips to the side, squishing up her face. "Not myself. I would have never done that without tequila and blow job shots."

My heart sinks. Is she trying to tell me in a polite way that without her beer goggles on, she would have never been interested in me?

Of course she isn't, you ugly motherfucker. She's so far above your paygrade, you couldn't touch her if you were standing on a twelve-foot ladder.

No strings.

I suddenly hate that fucking expression. Yes there are fucking strings. The strings are, I don't ever want to see you with another man. That *no fraternization policy* goes double for you, little sister.

There's an unreadable squint in her left eye, and my palpitations kick up a notch. I have to keep things professional. She's not just a counselor, she's gonna be working with Hailey.

I'm frozen, mute, hands in my pockets, dick hard, brain shutting down...

Then, she fucking saves me, poking at my chest, her eyelashes fluttering, a little glitter catching the light on her cheeks as she says, "Did you know you were going to be my boss?"

"No." I finally form words, then clarify. "Not until I spotted the Camp WanderLust t-shirt in your bag."

She nods, chewing the corner of her mouth, tapping the toes of her floral-patterned hiking boots. "So, where do you want me?"

I grunt as my cock finds a new inch it didn't have before. I want to tell her I *want* her everywhere. Right here, right now. In my office. Under the stars. In her cabin.

And that teasing sparkle in her wide, eat-me-alive-eyes tells me she knows what she's doing to me.

I grind my molars and growl through clenched teeth, "I need to introduce you to someone."

* * *

"This is Hailey," I tell Summer as we come into the activity room, and the way her face lights up almost makes me crumble. "She's the young girl we hired you for, as a speech therapist."

Her hands clasp in front of her mouth.

Hailey turns at the sound of her name, the finger painting she's up to her elbows in forgotten, and raises her hand in a quick salute, leaving a stripe of purple and yellow paint on her forehead.

"Where you been, Papa Pwice?" Hailey squishes up her nose. "You said you would paint wif me."

Hailey called me just Price for the first year after we met, which was fine by me. Then she started putting the 'papa' in front. Someday, maybe she'll drop the 'Price' but whatever works for her. She's not had the easiest path in her six short years, so I promised myself above all else, I won't do anything that makes it harder.

The salute is something my dad and I used to do when I was a kid before he disappeared, leaving me and my brother with my mom, who had no business raising kids.

Weird how the past comes back to the present, even when you wish it wouldn't. Hailey clasps her paint-covered hands together like she's saying a prayer, an excited sparkle in her eyes as she says, "I made it to the top of da rope today wif Miss Wiley!" she bursts out with her cute as fuck little lisp, then turns to Summer. "Who are you?"

"This is Summer," I say, her name as sweet as honey on my tongue.

Miss Wiley is Monica Wiley, my accountant and assistant, and the closest thing I have to a mother and a stand-in grandmother to Hailey. I begged her and paid her a boat load of cash to come with us this summer as a 'counselor', but really I just needed a friendly face and someone I trusted besides Ted to help me with Hailey.

"Thummer..." Hailey squints and nods. "I wike your name."

"Thanks," Summer smiles on a soft laugh. "I like yours too."

"She's going to be helping you. You remember we talked about what a speech therapist is?"

"I wemember." Hailey nods, scratching at her cheek,

leaving another paint smudge behind, and my heart sings whenever I see her smile. "She's nice. I wike her."

With that, she's done with me and goes back to her painting. I turn, Summer's eyes narrow and I already know what she is thinking.

"My daughter," I exhale, my heart breaking at the flicker of shock and pain in her warm brown eyes, feeling the unusual need to explain. "I didn't really know her mom. Tequila was involved," I say, and her face softens in understanding. "I'm not proud of how it happened, but I'm proud to be her father. She's changed everything for me."

Summer rolls her lips, her eyes drifting to the bank of windows across the room where there are other staff outside, standing in groups, doing the social things I never seem to understand.

My heart is racing as her silence ends with, "No chance of you and her mom ever…?"

I shake my head. "No. Was never like that and she passed away. It's just me and Hailey."

"Oh, God, I'm sorry. I—" Horror and embarrassment send a shadow across her soft features.

"It's okay. I've never been great with people, but with Hailey we're muddling through this whole parenting thing together. She's probably raising me more than I'm raising her. I want her to have this." I wave my arm in an arc, but Summer blinks, looking unsure. "Nature. Adventure. She spent her first years in Chicago. The city never worked for me."

Some part of me wants to tell her more, about the jagged and jaded parts. She's too soft. Too pure. I don't want her to carry around the broken parts of me. Or the reasons why I'm that way.

"You don't like the city," she says, and it's not a question, so I don't answer. "I grew up in New York until I was seven, then we moved to Detroit. That's about as city as you get. I still go back to New York whenever I can. I love it there." I see in the way her eyebrows rise, the way her lips stay open. I'm missing some cue here, but whatever it is, I'm lost. As much as my heart and my dick want to spend time with Summer, what I want will always be second to what Hailey needs.

"You should get to know her," I say, wondering if such a perfect, sweet girl like her could ever understand the monsters inside of me and why they came to live there. "See you later."

* * *

They don't know I'm watching them.

The view from the camera in the living room of our cabin shows me the back of my daughter's head, her blonde hair curling around her ears as she sits with Summer on the floor next to the wide back window, repeating lines of a silly made-up rhyme that has her giggling as much as talking.

The entire camp has cameras and audio equipment

set up. The Adventure Network installed it all, wanting to get a realistic flavor of my life.

Side benefit I didn't expect is I get to be a fucking voyeur. I'm the watcher instead of the watched, for once.

From my seat behind the monitors in the office in the main hall, I take it all in. Summer is a fucking natural with Hailey, making the whole thing into a game, and if I didn't want to admit it to myself before, I'm beginning to understand what other people mean when they talk about how it feels to fall in love.

The falling part is spot on. Like falling down a sheer mountainside with no fucking helmet.

Still, all I can keep thinking is, she's perfect.

She's sweet and sassy and smart. With perfect hair. Perfect tits. Perfect ass. And don't get me started on those lips.

Inside my head, there are not just visions of the filthy, monstrous things I want to do with her and to her.

But other things. Things I was sure would never mean anything to me.

Like waking up next to someone every morning. Making sure she eats and drinks and goes to the doctor and never uses her phone while she's driving.

But that's not the most shocking thing going on inside my head.

I can't shake the feeling I want to give Hailey a sibling. Or ten. With this girl who is rocking my boat until I feel like I'm going to puke over the edge.

Fuck. I know she's a city girl. I see the painted nails,

the makeup, the beauty-salon smooth legs. I'm all wrong for her, but she's my goddess and I would die a happy man if I just got to taste that pussy one time.

No fraternization with the staff.

Even if I'd recognized Summer the moment I saw her, I don't think I would have been able to stop myself from being pulled into her orbit. I couldn't have walked away.

My phone starts ringing, and I grab it without hesitating, grateful for the fucking distraction from the chaos inside my head and the fist squeezing at my heart.

It's Ted.

I answer in my usual baseline irritated tone. "What?"

He chuckles, knowing me well enough to realize my surly demeanor is nothing personal. "Good to hear your voice too, *dick*. How are things going?"

I turn the volume back on and my balls seize up as Summer stumbles over her own made-up tongue twister. *Six suckers sucking syrup surely sucks.* Her laugh doesn't help. I'd like to hear that laugh while she's sucking my syrup.

"Fine. What do you need?"

"Look, I know you've got Hailey there and a million and one things to do… but the Adventure Network guy wants us to do a hike up the north logging road to the original camp cabin with some of the staff tomorrow, but no one's been up there for about a month. Need to be sure it's still standing and get it cleaned up a little. Never know if a bear's been for a visit or who knows what. Can you get up there and make sure it's ready while I manage the staff training here? You're more the handle-the-shit-in-the-woods guy and I'm the handle-the-paperwork-and-the-humans guy."

"I do not disagree with that," I mutter, trying to catch my breath.

All other thought is dampened by Summer slowly pronouncing the word 'suck' over and over, sounding it out slowly like she's been sent here by Satan to torture me.

Or tempt me.

"Great," Ted says over the sound of voices in the background. "Wiley and I will take care of Hailey."

"Fine. I'll check it out."

"You can go most of the way in your Jeep, the road is rougher now though, but you'll make it. The last few hundred yards you'll be on foot."

Yeah, and I won't be alone.

Chapter Seven

Price

It's late-afternoon by the time Summer and I get to the end of the logging road. There was paperwork to handle, and a long fucking meeting with the TV people, followed by me trying to calm Ted down when they said they were still preparing the preliminary paperwork on the offer.

It's just a game. They want my name as much as Ted wants their money. I could give a shit, except I want the camp to succeed. I want it to be home for Hailey and securing this deal not only helps Ted keep his life savings, but puts enough zeros in my bank account that I know Hailey will be taken care of, no matter what.

Even with all that on my mind, it's the way

Summer's fleshy thighs taunt me from the passenger seat that has me nearly running us off the side of the road. The way her tits jiggle and bounce with every bump are making this feel like the longest drive in history.

The road turns to a series of deep wash outs and I ease the Jeep forward as far as the road will take us, down shifting as I steer to the side on a patch of grass and dirt, the brakes whining as I bring us to a stop.

"We're going to have to walk the rest of the way." Marking the trail ahead is a pile of boulders, with an overgrown path just beyond leading to the north toward the cabin.

"Walk?" She turns in her seat, her brows pulled together as I squeeze my jaw, trying to fight off the smile as I wonder where in the hell you would buy a pair of floral embroidered hiking boots. "Into the woods?"

"Adventure camp." I shrug. "You did read the job description when you applied, right?"

She nods, tension in her shoulders. "When you said we were going to check on a cabin, I didn't realize I was going to end up a contestant on Survivor." Her voice wavers between excitement and fear, then she turns with that dimple showing and adds, "Or, Naked and Afraid. I love that show."

Jesus. Just hearing her say the word naked has my nuts tightening.

"You'll be okay. City is way more dangerous than what's out here. You have more survival skills than you give yourself credit for." I pull at the door handle, swing my legs out the open door and hop down onto the uneven hard dirt ground.

We talked mainly about Hailey on the ride, both of us keeping things light as I did my best to not navigate the Jeep down the drop offs on either side of the barely passable road. But I need to man up here. She had my dick in her mouth last night. There are things that need discussing.

Stay strong, I remind myself, and grit my teeth.

"Yeah, we should talk," I say, glancing up through the streaming streaks of muted light coming through the trees. The sky is darkening like my mood. I'm unsure how to start a discussion about what happened and what can and can't happen from here. My heart and my head are at war, and in the middle are Hailey and Summer.

I grab my backpack out of the back of the jeep, her eyes popping wide when she sees my hunting rifle strapped to the bottom.

"Just in case," I say, grabbing her smaller pack and easing it onto her shoulders, the creamy flesh of her neck calling for my teeth.

"Okay. Is that why you wanted me to come? So, we could...*talk?*" She adds a little eyebrow bob and an unsure swallow, that teasing look returning, making heat rake over my skin.

"That's right." I square my shoulders, reaching out to flick my green carabiner that's clipped to her beltloop, my heart speeding knowing she's wearing something of mine. We exchange a look as I turn and step toward the path, easing her next to me with my hand on the small of her back just under her bite-sized pack I filled with a trail mix, bug spray and a couple canteens full of water.

Almost like I was planning a fucking picnic.

Mine is twice the size. I'm always prepared, so I've got more food, water, filtration tabs, blanket and first aid supplies. And my gun.

I shrug, feeling the weight of more than what I'm physically carrying right now. But as I'm well aware—as are the million subscribers to my channel—things can go wrong in a blink, and there's more at stake now than just my hide.

As the brush closes behind us, a sheer wind cuts through the woods. Our feet crunch on the leaves and sticks as we move forward.

The trail is only wide enough for us to walk single file, and I shift to the front, feeling a loss at not having the privilege of keeping my eyes on her ass in those shorts. But I'll always make sure where she goes is safe, so I go first.

I may be a thrill seeker and a danger addict, but I'm scared to death. I have to use my words to navigate a complicated situation where my heart is involved on both sides, and other parts of me are making their own demands.

But when it comes to Hailey. I made promises to myself about how her life would be. No distractions. No possible evil step-women in her life.

My boot makes a squishing sound as I look down

and ahead to see where the recent rain has left a muddy wash. I reach behind me. "Watch your step there, the ground is soft. Give me your hand."

She slips her tiny hand into my massive one without question or hesitation, and warmth shoots up my arm. Once I lead her through the muck, I step ahead again, the tension in my center more than just about her safety.

"So, what do you need to talk to me about?" She breaks through the uneasy silence. Her voice chipper and optimistic, making me feel more like a complete ass for what I need to say.

"What happened with us."

"Oh?" Her voice rises, and thoughts of slipping my tongue through her folds and up to that tight little asshole assault me from all sides. "Is there an us?"

"No." The word comes out as a kind of guttural sound, and I clear my throat, trying to remember what I need to say and why I need to say it. "I mean, I want that, but things are complicated."

"Because you have a daughter."

I swallow the rock lodged in my throat, the breeze rustling the leaves overhead like a warning for me to tread lightly, but I don't know how. "No, not just that."

Her smile makes me feel like I'm walking through broken glass, then she adds, "Hailey us a jewel. You're doing a great job raising her. She's amazing."

Fuck, please don't make this harder. "She likes you too. But—"

Before I finish, she's stomping by me, tossing me an excited look and rushing ahead.

I follow her with my eyes, the view of her stalling my heartbeat for a moment as the trailhead opens, and the cabin comes into view in a small clearing.

"Oh, wow! Like Goldilocks and the three bears." She skip-runs ahead of me, then squeals as the sky opens up, rain starting to pelt her as she runs. I curse under my breath as I sprint to catch up. "Come on, I'll race you!"

"*No.* Summer, wait, you have no idea what's..." I growl as I adjust my pack. She's got short little legs, but they are churning, and she's way more nimble than my oafish size allows. "*Wait!*"

With the place sitting empty, it could have new residents. Ones that would find her an easy target.

She laughs as I stumble, swearing and righting myself on a thick pine tree. Then she turns, running backwards, lowering her voice to a rough grumble. "Who's been sleeping in *my* bed?"

Rain soaks me through, and Summer as well, her green t-shirt clinging to her every curve as the cold shower barely dampens the heat rising from my skin.

The field around the structure is overgrown. There could be snakes, hidden potholes just waiting to break her ankle, ticks and stagnant water carrying disease...

She's plowing forward, so I need to catch up. I drop my pack to the ground by another huge boulder and force my legs to go faster. I'm on her as she reaches the front door, and she slaps her palms against it.

"I win!" She huffs breathlessly, spinning around to light me up with a killer smile and that heart-stopping dimple.

"Don't." I reach forward, snatching her wrist and tugging her off balance toward me as the rain soaks us both. "You need to listen."

My rough manner does nothing to dampen her playful mood. She could put a shine on the dullest day.

"Spoilsport." She shrugs, blowing the water from her lips, flattening herself back against the door where a slight overhang offers some shelter. Her exposed skin sparkles even through the rain, another reminder of how different our lives are. I didn't even know that glitter body lotion existed, and manicures don't last long in the wilderness. "I was fine. There's no one here."

I fish the key out of my pocket, swinging the padlock upward and slipping the key into the slot. It clicks open as I tug, the metal clinking as I pull it from the metal loop and swing open the latch. "I'm going in first. How often have you been to a deserted cabin the woods?"

"Uhhh, never," she answers with a nonchalant smirk.

"Just, there's danger where you don't expect it. And you don't even know to expect it." The hard edge in my voice masks my own fear that something could hurt her. Take her away from me. "Come. Inside. Now."

"Okay, big brother. You're the boss, *take me* inside." She quirks a brow and her cheeks turn pink against the cooling rain.

"Summer..." My resolve is being tested. "It's Hailey and the camp and..." I'm at a loss. I have no idea how to explain the turmoil inside me. "No fraternization. Remember?"

She cocks a brow. "You got all your fraternization out of your system last night?"

It sounds ridiculous even to me. What I want to tell her is the first time I saw her, I wanted to marry her. I never in my life thought of having a wife, but when she's around, nothing make sense and at the same time, everything feels right.

I kick open the door as a roll of thunder rumbles and a flash of lightning punches through the sky.

Inside, we're both dripping on the bare wood floor as she peels her soaking backpack off and tosses it out the front door onto the small porch, as I silently run through all the reasons I shouldn't have brought her here, but none of them seem to make much of a difference. Because being here, with her, I'm in so far over my head, I can't even see straight.

Inside, the damp, closed-up, musty smell mixes with Summer's sweet cherry scent, making my heart thump in a primal drumbeat.

"You know that will never last, right?" she asks as I step into the small, dark space, shaking the water from my hair as I grab the crank light hanging on the wall next to the door and turn the handle in frantic circles until the dim yellow bulb illuminates the room. "The no fraternization thing, I mean. People are people, and you have a bunch of twenty-somethings stuck in wood shacks for the summer. Things are gonna happen. Nature takes its course, whether you want it to or not—*ahhhhh!*" Her chirpy speech turns to a scream as she stumbles back, a single finger pointed at the small window above the makeshift sink.

I drop the light, and it rolls like a spinning siren across the rough wood floor. Summer scurries next to me, tucking herself to my side in abject terror as I stare across the room, trying to figure out what's scared her.

"What?" I say hoarsely, squinting toward where her finger points.

"There! *Right there!*" she's practically climbing me like a tree now, to which I have zero objections except I hate to see her frightened. So much so, the same sort of anger I had when I found out Hailey was being bullied at school starts to rise inside me.

As the light on the floor rocks back and forth, I catch the shimmering, undeniable pattern of an intricate web slung between the window and a shelf next to the sink. In the center, there's the distinctive shape of a fairly impressive wolf spider.

"Spiders are the devil," she hisses as I ease her off my side, grabbing a piece of kindling left near the cast-iron wood stove and sweeping it through the outer strands of the web, wrapping it like cotton candy on the end of the stick, encasing the spider in its own web.

I spin on my boot, heading toward the door as she races in an arc around me to the faded brown sofa, jumping onto the center cushion. "What are you going to do with it?"

I shrug on a frown. "Put her outside. She's not here to hurt you. I'm not going to kill her, just rehome her."

"Her? How do you know it's a her?"

I hold up the stick into the light as I pull the door open, seeing the inch-wide spider frantically trying to free herself from her own prison. "Females are bigger. A male wouldn't be this big." I gently toss the piece of wood out the door, knowing the rain will actually help release the web from around the spider, and she will make her way to safety somewhere else.

"Jesus. I do not belong out in the woods." She shakes her head, palming the water back into her hair off her forehead, the ends of her braids seeping water in two points just above each of her tits. "New York rats I can take, but not spiders."

I do a quick walk, poking my head into the small bedroom, making sure there are no uninvited guests, then unlock the metal cabinet that stows a small amount of food and water.

Summer falls with a bounce on her ass in the center of the sofa, crossing her ankle over her knee and working the laces loose on both her boots before setting them on the floor.

She wiggles, tucking her legs up under her perfect ass and watching me as I wander around like I'm lost.

I need to do the one thing I don't want to do. Tell her this can't happen. "Summer...it's just...we can't—" I start, not knowing how to continue. What I need to say feels like daggers in my throat.

"Tell me something. What is it about me that you don't like?"

"There's absolutely nothing about you I don't like. You're perfect. You're—"

"Is it that I'm a city girl? I hate spiders, and you give them new homes? You could survive at the top of Mt. Fuji with a popsicle stick and some Tic Tacs. What happened to make you hate the city? Were your parents hippies, and you're some anti-establishment adventure junkie?" She finishes in a breathy huff as I search for a way to explain.

"No." I draw a ragged breath, working my way back to her, scooping the crank light up off the floor and whipping the handle around until the light perks up. Maybe the only way through this is to tell her the things I want to forget. The things that made me promise to give Hailey a different life than I had. "My father was in the army. We traveled, he drank, but things were okay. Mom was sort of never really there. My dad wasn't the warmest guy, and later, after he was injured and left the army, he was less than warm."

She scoots over in an invitation for me to sit, her eyes as welcoming as her mouth was last night.

"And?" she says, resting her elbow on the back of the sofa, leaning her head against her palm so she's facing me as I drop onto the cushion next to her, the entire sofa popping up off the floor when I do. It's taking everything

I have to fight the urge to pin her down and have a feast between her legs. "What's this city prejudice you have all about?"

Rain sprays against the windows sounding like a sea of pebbles trying to come through. The walls vibrate with the cracking thunder and white flashes of lightning cast shadows across the flawless skin of her face.

"We moved to Philly. I found out about being hungry and how mean whiskey can make someone." I scratch my fingers over my jaw on a long exhale. "Short version, Dad left, Mom went off the rails. Whenever we stayed with Dad, there was a new step-mother. None of them good. My brother was ten, I was sixteen, when we moved into an even shittier part of the city with my mom, after Dad's newest wife decided she wanted them to start their own family and we didn't fit in. I was the man of the house, but I couldn't protect my brother. Our house was robbed more than once. Within a couple years, my brother was running the streets. Mom was checked out. The city ate them both up and nothing I did changed anything."

I palm my forehead, squeezing my temples with one hand as I rest my other on her knee like that connection is going to help me somehow. I don't think I've said so many words in a row in decades.

Summer nods. "You lost a lot but the city didn't take it."

I don't indulge in memories of the past often, and the uneasy tightness around my throat reminds me why. I don't know what to do with emotion besides act out. It makes me want to punch and break things. That's why I've distracted myself with dangerous activities. It doesn't leave any room for remembering.

"What happened to your brother? You talk to him still?" Summer asks as I keep my eyes focused on nothing facing forward.

"A stray bullet. Came through our front fucking window. Nick died before the ambulance even got there."

I look to see her fingers pressed to her mouth, eyes welling, but she doesn't say anything and I appreciate her silence.

"Out here," I explain, "I can protect Hailey. I know the dangers, and I know how to prepare for them, how to fight them. I've spent my whole life doing that. But the city is chaos. There's no order to it. No honor. No hierarchy. It makes no sense to me."

Another bolt of lightning cuts through the sky over the tree tops. In the bright flash, I catch a dark shape out the window lumbering around in front of the cabin.

Fuck, my pack is out there. I was so fucking turned around when she ran, I left it.

As the thunder shakes the house, Summer hunches over, hands looping behind her neck.

"You okay with storms?" I ask, keeping my eyes on the movement outside, giving her knee a soft squeeze.

"I'm okay so long as I'm not out in them." She peeks

up from her crouched position. "We'll wait here until it passes, right?"

Daylight has turned into dusk under the storm clouds. "Yeah—" I start, but she cuts me off.

"*What the hell is that?*" she shrieks, pointing again at the window, only this time, I know it's not just a spider. A series of three lightning flashes illuminate the sky, the woods, and the hulking bear rises onto her feet about fifty feet from the front of the cabin, sniffing the air as three smaller versions of her toddle along behind.

Instinct has me pulling Summer against me. Her soft to my hard. Her fear to my protective fury.

I take a deep breath of her. Leaning in to her damp hair, resting my chin on her head, wondering in some way, if this could work.

"It's a bear," I say. "Black bear. Not that mean, but not that nice either. Especially because she's got cubs."

"Aww, babies?" She pushes up on her knees, trying to get a better look.

"They're cute, but with them here she'll be aggressive." I clear my throat, not sure how to say what I have to say next. "And my pack was out there. I dropped it to catch up with you. I had food and water in there, and my gun. So, I just provided mom and her cubs with a meal."

Summer hunches into me, and I don't try to stop her. Somehow, telling her about the past, explaining why I have to put Hailey first, has drained any fight that was left in me. Somehow, it's made me want her more, not less.

As her body snugs against mine, my traitorous dick responds, and all the reasons I should push her away toddle off like the baby bears into the storm.

Her stomach let's out a loud growl in the beat of silence and she snorts.

"You need food," I say, pissed again that I left our supplies outside to be ravaged by a single mom and her triplets.

"I'm okay."

"What did you have for breakfast?" I clear my throat, looking down to see her cock a half smile, with a sultry lick of her lips and a glance at my lap. "The Black Swan have a continental breakfast buffet for you?"

"I wish. The last thing I had to eat was…" She clicks her teeth together, wiggling her index finger at my lap.

* * *

There isn't much food in the storage cabinet, which doesn't surprise me. Even with a locked metal cabinet, a starving determined bear could take down the door or come through the window and help themselves easily if they caught a good scent.

I find a couple sealed jars of peanut butter. Crunchy, thank God. Some tea bags in a glass jar and four cans of Spaghetti O's.

Hailey's favorite.

Summer watches from where I lifted her onto the small countertop to sit as I work wood into the belly of the stove, adding enough oxygen to get it to catch, then working the rusty can opener on the Spaghetti O's.

The storm is still doing its thing in rumbles and flashes, but until there's more light outside and enough time for the bears to finish off whatever they discovered in my pack, we're stuck.

That's not the only reason I want to keep her here. We're alone, together, and my only other worry is Hailey, but if she's with Ted and Wiley, she won't miss me at all. They'll have her knee deep in s'mores and grape soda until she passes out.

Within a few minutes, I've got the canned noodle concoction bubbling in a cast-iron skillet, the tea pot whistling as I hand Summer the jar of peanut butter and a spoon from the single drawer under the counter.

"That's your appetizer," I say as I point toward the little two-seat wood table. "Not exactly a feast," I warn as I put the weird meal down on the top and Summer hops down from the counter to take a seat. The cabin has warmed with the fire, and our damp clothes have nearly dried. "Sorry. My culinary skills could do with some refinement."

She laughs, but shakes her head. "Peanut butter straight from the jar? And, it's *crunchy?* I'm in heaven."

Picking up a spoon, she digs into the peanut butter first. Then, the Spaghetti O's as I pour the hot water into a mug and dangle a tea bag inside.

Every time there's a flash of lightning, I check

outside. I've seen the bears twice more, and I can hear them with my trained ears.

What I'm really worried about is that it will soon be dropping dark for real. With those bears around, it's not safe to try to get back to the Jeep, which means we're here until morning.

And, there's only one bed.

Chapter Eight

Price

Having Summer out here in the woods with me, my ever-present tension seems to lift. I'm still not sure why a girl like her would look twice at a grumpy, lumbering single dad like me, but we're here and something about feeding her and the way she makes me want to actually talk is making me think there's room in mine and Hailey's life for her after all.

My brain's been fried since she wrapped her lips around me, calling me Daddy with those big doe eyes. My promises to myself about keeping it just Hailey and me are beginning to waver.

I talked to her about things I haven't thought of since

I was a kid. This sparkly city girl somehow draws out parts of me I thought I'd long put away forever.

I asked her about herself. She said she's going to New York in the fall and when I heard that, my heart turtled back up, and I had to take a moment telling her I was going to check the bedroom for spiders before I settled her in for the night.

She bought that, but I've been in here too long and the sight of the single bed has my resolve cracking.

I grab the door handle and swing open to door to find her standing there, fist hovering, ready to knock.

"Your room is clear. No spiders."

I bite back my groan when I see she's stripped off her damp clothes and wrapped herself in one of the blankets we keep in a cedar chest that doubles as a coffee table in front of the sofa.

"I didn't want to sleep in wet clothes," she says, her eyes suddenly shy as I rake my gaze up and down her fertile body.

"God, you are beautiful." I can't help myself. Her sweet round face is what will fill my dreams for the rest of my life. I want what's under that blanket more than I want to breathe.

I swear I smell her arousal too, as my own lust and emotion crash around inside me. I throw all the reasons this can't happen into the belly of the burning stove.

"One bed," she says on an unsteady breath.

The thrumming need to take her is beating on me like a hammer to the balls. She's pure and sweet and soft, and I'm none of those things, but it doesn't stop me from reaching out and grabbing her around the waist with both hands. Her squeak is not fear but surprise, as her lips fall open and everything in my life makes sudden sense as I crush my mouth to hers.

Sexual hunger crowds out any other doubts. With every passing second, this girl turns me inside out, pulling emotions from me no matter how much I try to avoid them.

I press my body against hers, letting her feel what she's doing to me as the warmth of her mouth welcomes my tongue, and all I can think about is how the dewy flesh between her legs might taste.

My breathing turns violent as I pull away, taking a bite of her lower lip as I go, pulling it outward while I spin her toward the bed, releasing her lip as I shove her harder than I should onto the red and yellow striped blanket that covers the lumpy mattress.

All the years of denial and the flatline of my emotions rush out of me as I strip my shirt, watching her eyes round as she comes to settle like an offering in front of me.

"Lose the blanket and spread your legs." I narrow my eyes, my breathing coming faster, faster.

Shyness takes her for a beat, but it's quickly washed away by the lust in her eyes as I reach forward and press her knees wide while she untucks the blanket and opens it, leaving her naked and exposed in all her perfection.

For every dangerous mountain and freezing blizzard

I've survived, nothing has ever felt as victorious as having this stunning creature open herself to me, and my cock hardens as white spots flicker in my vision.

My fingers twitch, wanting to feel the round flesh of her tits in my hands. Outside of the moment I met my daughter, nothing has affected me the way her sexy, bare cunt is affecting me right now.

Even from here, I know she's tight. But I also know she's mine, and the edge I've been on since leaving her in her room last night snaps.

I want to ravage her, but I also want to take my time. Enjoy every inch, taste her in long slow strokes until she explodes in my mouth.

The anticipation beats inside of me, but I know even when I get my first taste, feel her body take me deep, I'll only truly be at peace when her body is full of me. Round with proof of who she belongs to from now until forever.

I drop onto the bed, caging her as my dick rages, but I ignore him for now as I draw a peaked nipple into my mouth, taking my time, reveling in the texture, the way the flesh firms against my tongue. She arches as I move to the other breast, gripping the flesh until she hisses and her savory scent calls to me. I shift back, dropping to my knees on the floor, tugging her lush body to the edge of the bed.

"This will be mine. Once I lick you here, Daisy, your brother owns this cunt, do you understand?"

"Yes, brother."

That's all I hear as I drop my mouth to latch onto her pussy, thrusting my tongue as deep as her tightness allows, as she bows off the bed.

"Oh, fuck, *Daddy*."

That word makes the world stop spinning. She used it once last night, and it had the same effect it's having now.

Madness takes root inside me as I split her sex with my tongue, running it up and down, then suckling on that hard nub until it feeds me what I demand.

Her eyes are squeezed shut as I inhale her feminine scent and her flavor coats my throat.

I suck and release, applying pressure with my tongue, back and forth, over and over until her thick thighs tighten on the sides of my head.

"Oh my God." Her quaking voice matches her quivering flesh. "Right there. Oh God, don't stop. Right. There."

I will bow to her pleasure always, but soon she will understand even if she told me to stop, taking my tongue from her heaven right now would be impossible.

Her ripe scent fills my nose as her wetness streams into my eager mouth. My eyes nearly roll all the way back when her orgasm takes hold and I ease a finger into her soaking opening, priming her for what's coming.

I'm like a dog in heat, my dick wants in there and won't be denied any longer. I ease my face back, working my finger in and out as her pussy undulates around the thick digit, my finger making wet sounds as her climax takes flight and my obsession grows.

No more fucking my fist for relief. My dick will be home inside of her every day.

I already know, letting her go will never happen. I'd never recover. I will claim her, spill inside her, show her what her life will be like filled with me from now on.

She rocks and twists, hips bucking, fingers extended, then a second later, tugging at the bedding with desperate sobs, telling me she's close to breaking.

"Wet and ready to be fucked, aren't you, sis?"

Her virgin opening softens only slightly as I pump my thick finger in and out, doing what I can to stretch her so the pain might be less when she takes me. As she tumbles down from her orgasm, her lust-blind eyes find mine.

"You'll be begging for Daddy's mouth from now on, won't you?"

I keep my eyes on her pussy, barely able to look away from its beauty as she makes some moaning sounds of agreement from above. Her body answers me as much as her moans.

"You'll be begging for cock, too. You'll be greedy for it. Greedy to show me all your slutty tricks."

My dirty words initiate another gush of her nectar until it's dripping down my hand.

"That was crazy." She throws her forearm over her face, her body flushed and pink.

"Things are going to get crazier. Because that big

cock you sucked so well last night is going in here next." I displace my middle finger from her opening, then drive it back into her sloppy wetness as her walls clutch and the entry point of resistance makes her gasp.

The scent of her willing pussy has my dick as rigid as a red oak. I've not made use of my equipment as most males, but I know it's no easy chore to take my length and girth, especially for a fresh, untouched paradise.

Her flavor courses through me, and I've never tasted anything so incredible. I'm close to dumping my seed in my pants, but the thought of not planting myself inside her is offensive to me.

I unleash my erection, stripping my lower body in jerky, angry movements until I'm naked, climbing on top of Summer, ready to claim that cherry she's been teasing me with like a dimpled brat.

My heart pounds as I guide my throbbing cock to her opening, as her hands slip around my neck the same way they did last night, pulling my mouth to hers, cracking my heart wide open.

I've never felt connected to another human like I feel with her. Outside of Hailey, but that's a different playing field all together.

Her hands caress my neck as she takes my tongue, her body wet and willing as I find the slick heat of her opening and push.

So fucking tight.

I freeze as her fingernails dig into my flesh, but

instead of pain, it's fueling the building pleasurable pressure ready to erupt from my balls.

Her opening has a choke-hold on my dick. The beat of fear thumping inside me that I'm the one causing her pain has me ready to retreat.

She reads my reticence instantly, breaking our kiss with shallow warm breaths against my cheek.

"Give it to me, Daddy." Her whispered words are the pistol that propels me off the blocks.

I work my thick head into her opening, the hiss of her pain lancing my heart as I bind us together, keeping my eyes on hers as I become the man she will know forever as her first. Her last. Her everything and always.

"You'll be wet for me for the rest of your life. When I want you, you'll be ready for me, won't you?"

The question seems to distract her for a moment from the pain. Her throaty moans and the arch of her back has me releasing the monstrous hunger she's created inside me.

"So big," she moans through clenched teeth, her eyes squeezing shut.

I ease back, then pump forward as her walls constrict, her moans turning to sharp yelps as I cradle her head, running my thumbs over her hot cheeks.

"This is what you do to me. You've created a beast that wants to breed. The drive to get as close to you as two humans can is unrelenting," I growl in fevered bursts of truth. "You feel so fucking good. Daddy hates hurting you. Just let me in, sis. I promise I'll make you feel so good. The pain will be over soon."

Daddy. Fucking Daddy. That word has my hips churning, my heart exploding as I bear down, dropping my face to her neck, licking and kissing and biting, wanting all of her all at once in every way I can muster.

Fucking her is the most intense and meaningful thing I've ever done. She grinds against me as I buck into her clenching hole, the muscles pulsing around my dick.

I'm claiming her with my cock and my mouth, and soon, after just a few more pumps, with my seed.

"That cherry you teased me with belongs to me now," I say as I lick around the shell of her ear, my strokes turning slow and steady, long and deep, as the bed squeals in protest under the demands of my weight.

"Yes, big brother took my cherry," she moans as I thrust into her warmth, my face in front of hers, nose to nose, breath to breath as I pick up the pace again, biting the inside of my cheek to keep from erupting.

"Yeah, he did. And he licked you too. Admit you wanted your brother to do that. Say you liked how I licked that tight little pussy."

Her mouth falls into an O, her inner muscles massaging my length, pulling the seed from my balls. I'm going to come in a fury. An unstoppable wave of pleasure that's coming from the deepest places in my soul.

"Yes. I liked it. I wanted it."

"I know you did. I'm going to feast on you whenever

I please. When I tell you I'm hungry, you'll open those legs for me without question, understand?"

She nods as her eyes roll back, and I reach between our sweat-slick bodies to find that swollen nub with my thumb. I start to circle, holding myself up on one locked arm, flesh slapping as I grind my teeth.

"You're going to make me cum inside you. Your pussy is begging for it. You did this, little girl, you did this to Daddy. Now you're going to take what I give you."

Her walls cinch around me, the filthy words have her gushing over my greedy dick as her body does the work of pulling the spend from my balls.

"Oh, God...Price. Brother. Daddy..."

Her orgasm lights mine as she thrashes and twists, and I thrust myself deep.

"You're taking it, baby. So good. Fucking tight, take it, take it..."

The orgasm rages through me. Through every cell in my body as my roars rattle the windows. At the last moment, I grab her legs, pulling them wide as I push forward, dragging her pelvis upward as I drive myself down. Her orgasm only urges me on, and my last grinding pumps are savage. I know I'm being too rough with her innocent body, but the way she's screaming and flooding the bed, I guess my little dimpled princess likes things a little rough.

I'm blinded by the pleasure of my seed spurting into her depths. I cum as she comes down, her tight warmth welcoming what I'm giving, my balls clenched, pumping, pumping, pumping every drop into her womb.

I drop onto her soft body, letting her legs fall, my face nuzzling her neck as her soft breasts press against my chest.

I thrust in and out, small, soft movements letting her body milk me of every drop. The feeling of belonging she gives me is new. How Summer has done this to me so fast, I don't understand, but I do know she's never getting away.

How our different lives can come together, I'm not sure, but in this moment none of that matters.

Peace comes over me for the first time in my life as her hands wrap around my neck, pulling me down in a soft, comforting gesture, as exhaustion takes me. How she's changed me doesn't seem possible, but I feel it down into my marrow.

"I think you just fraternized inside me." Her warm breath teases my ear, and another spurt of cum finds its way inside her.

"Yes, and there's more where that came from, baby. I hope you're ready. Because big brother is never going to get enough of this pussy. Never."

Chapter Nine

Summer

"Hey, anyone in there?" A voice cuts through the comforting thump of Price's heartbeat as I sit bolt upright. "Hey, Price!"

The warm orange and yellow sunrise peeks up over the trees out the window of the small bedroom, and there's the pluvial scent of the morning after the rain all around.

There's silence for a moment, as I stare into Price's narrowing green eyes. He eases his hand from behind my neck, slides out of the bed, stuffing his feet into his pants on a grumble.

I'm not sure how much we slept. Not a lot, and it's early. The night was incredible. Not just the sex but how rough and demanding and greedy he was one second, then so tender and attentive and concerned the next.

Losing your v-card to an overachieving boner like Price's has left me achy and sore, but the magic that man can do with his mouth?

I'd forget I had third degree burns with his face between my legs.

Which happened a lot. A. Lot.

Not the burns. The face. Between the legs.

"Get dressed." He leans over, planting a kiss on the top of my head, cupping my cheek in his rough palm. "Do as I say."

"Wait, but—" My words are lost as he stuffs his still half-hard cock behind his zipper, then heads through the door, swinging it half closed behind him after whisking his shirt off the floor in one long-armed swipe.

There's an impatient knock and the voice calling out again as I reluctantly push onto my knees, reaching out to touch the warm spot where I was tucked against the hardest, biggest chest in the world just a moment ago. His warmth is still on the sheets as I crawl to the edge of the bed and throw my legs over with a soft hiss, the pinpricks of pain in my newly deflowered lady bits reminding me to move gingerly.

Even in his bare feet, Price's footsteps make vibrating thuds through the floor, then the hinges of the front door let out a pained squeak.

I pull the rumpled blanket from the bed and tuck it around me. When Price went to the living room to get me some water after I nearly passed out from the rolling orgasms he insisted on giving me with his mouth after destroying my cherry, he hung my clothes near the wood stove on a chair to dry.

The same gruff male voice comes clearer now through the open door. "Price, hey, you okay?"

"Yeah. Good." Price grunts in his best monosyllabic caveman impression.

"Yeah, I see you're as talkative as ever. Ted called me. Said he didn't want to leave Hailey but needed someone to come up and check on you. Said you set off yesterday and didn't get back. No cell service up here, so people were worried. So, here I am."

"There was a bear," Price says as I tiptoe and inch along the wall of the bedroom, peeking around the doorframe to see the visitor dressed in an olive-green uniform and wearing a matching hat with a brass badge front and center. Price shoots a quick look over his shoulder as he slips his arms into his shirt, then says, "I... *we*....never mind. The bear had cubs with her. Came up to the door too."

"Yeah, I've seen her around on the trail cams and on our tracking. We tagged her a few years back. Named her Electra. She's not the friendliest as black bears go. She's got the personality of a grizzly. Good idea to stay put," the ranger says, his eyes catching me when I ease the door open a couple inches, smiling on a knowing nod toward Price, then lowering his voice, leaning in conspiratorially. "Ah, sorry man. Didn't pick up you were here with your girl."

Price's response comes faster than I expected, with a shake of his head. "No, just one of the camp counselors. Came up with me yesterday to check things out."

His denial sounds final. Decision made, and a darkness clouds around my heart.

"Fair enough. Your Jeep's okay, few branches down on the road from the storm though." Price nods in response. "I'll follow you back down. I've got a full can of bear spray just in case." He taps the spray can clipped to his belt. "Saw your pack out there. Bears had their way with it. Your rifle too. Looks like mama bear sat on it." He nods toward the contents of our packs strewn under the trees in front of the cabin. Then he leans to the right on a sly smile. "I'll wait over there. When you're ready, just holler."

* * *

"I didn't want that ranger knowing our business," Price explains as we head down the last section of the road, the Jeep hitting a pothole with a hard lurch. "People talk too much."

The ranger just split off onto another road in his truck ahead of us, leaving us to make the last bit of the ride back to the camp unescorted. I squeeze the remnants of the small pack I tossed on the porch last night. One strap is torn off and there's a new ragged opening down one side.

I feel the way it looks. The afterglow of the morning seems to have turned into the cold light of day.

I turn toward Price, noting the way he's gripping the steering wheel, the flex of his jaw muscle and the way the tendons on his neck are standing out.

I get why he feels he has to raise Hailey out here in the wilderness, and I get why he doesn't think I can be a part of that.

I wear glittery body lotion, and floral-embossed hiking boots. I have a standing salon appointment every Wednesday at noon. Outside of the boots I bought to come up here, ninety-nine percent of my shoes would be woefully inappropriate for even a walk on the grass in a park. I like heels and dresses and fussing over my magnetic lashes until they are perfect.

Besides, I've wanted to go to NYU since my sophomore year at Michigan State. I love New York. The noise and the smells and the fashion.

Speech therapy might not seem glamorous, but I love what I do and there's a lot of money to be made being a private therapist to the upper, upper class. It's what I've planned for almost three years.

I also know I pushed him last night. Taunted him really. Like I did that night after the bar.

He's a man, after all. He saw the opportunity and read the invitation and showed up ready for the party.

I got what I wanted, right? He destroyed my v-card, summer goal achieved.

"I get it," I finally choke out, trying not to say too much because my chin is starting to quiver.

"When we get back, there are some things I need to take care of. Then we'll talk. The parents are dropping off kids, I need to meet the network guys and—" He palms the wheel of the Jeep, turning under the tall carved log archway into Camp WanderLust. "I need to get some things sorted out. I know Hailey is going to rapid fire questions at me about why I was gone. I want to make sure she's okay."

Before we got in the Jeep to head out, Price had the ranger radio back to his headquarters and told them to call Ted and let him know we'd be back soon. Campers are arriving today so there's a lot to handle I'm sure.

I shrug. "Sounds good. I need to change clothes and get ready for another session with Hailey. Consistency is key with speech therapy. I know she'll be waiting for you. She comes first."

He opens his mouth. It hangs there like the words are frozen on his tongue, then he closes it without saying anything, only swallowing on a nostril-flaring inhale.

He doesn't know how to say what we both know needs to be said.

He told me this couldn't happen. And like an idiot, I thought that was negotiable.

But if I got what I wanted, why do I feel like pieces of my heart are scattered around my feet?

The next few minutes on the gravel road back into camp, Price accelerates like he's ready to be away from the tension that thickens the small interior of the Jeep.

"See ya," I say as casually as I can muster when he slows and parks the Jeep in front of the main hall. Counselors are waving as some early families pull in to drop off their kiddos for the next few weeks.

I grab the handle to the door and pull, swinging it open and hopping onto the ground before Price has the ignition off.

* * *

Hailey is a handful in the best sort of way. Her IQ has to be off the charts, but it's also her personality. She's forty years of wisdom and sass packed into a six-year-old's body.

The rest of the counselors were organized at tables checking in campers when we got back. I scooted off to my bunkhouse, jumped into a lukewarm shower, trying to wash away the clutching feeling in my chest along with Price's scent.

As I dressed, the reality of what we did came crashing down around me.

Raw. No condom.

Dumb. Dumb. Dumb.

It's been a few hours now, there's campers all around finding their way, and Ted asked me to stick by Hailey because the older woman that's her sort of nanny-ish stand-in grandmother, Wiley, is down with a migraine and Ted and Price have official new camp owner and TV network duties to tend to.

Hailey's been trying to teach me how to climb the rope in the outdoor obstacle course, scurrying up it like it's a ladder, then touching the branch it's attached to and inching back down. And I can tell how proud she is of keeping up with the exercises we were practicing yesterday, her 's' sounds much more sibilant as she repeats the tongue twister I taught her as she goes up and down the rope.

Funny, I sort of feel settled here. Not out of place with a desire for a Starbucks, or the sirens and twenty-four hour noise of the city.

I thought I wasn't the outdoors type, but here I am being taught to climb ropes by a six-year-old, and yesterday I went hiking in the wilderness. And I'm having fun doing it.

I did break a nail earlier today, and there was a quick twinge of angst that there's nowhere to go for a fix, but other than that, I'm getting downright outdoorsy.

Hailey waves at someone over my head, and I turn to see Price addressing a group of older kids by the start to the bigger obstacle course. His voice carries on the warmth of the summer breeze as he waves his thick arm toward a steep wooden wall with a knotted rope hanging down. He's covering rules and safety stuff, then, like magic, he's giving a quick demo of how to climb the wall.

In five effortless, hand over hand movements, he's

pulled his entire body weight up the rope, then flings himself over, falling onto his feet in a superhero landing on the other side, in a puff of dust.

The depth of his strength and skill leave me frozen and rapt as he comes around, wiping his hands down the front of his t-shirt, then claps three times, making a gesture for the campers to give it a try.

"Do you think my dad will mawwy you?" Hailey suddenly says, drawing my attention back to her.

I want to say no, because honestly, I think Price has made his choice and I know I should say no, but my tongue has a mind of its own. "How would you feel about that?"

"I'd wike it." She frowns. "Then you'd be my mom, sort of."

"Hailey." I crouch down to her level as she wipes at her eyes.

"I *do* have a mom already..."

"I know," I tell her. "Nobody can ever take that away."

"But you can have two moms, can't you?"

"You can. Lots of people do. But I think your dad wants it to just be the two of you for a while."

She shakes her head. "Uh uh. He wooks at you wike he wooks at me, except I'm his daughter. You're *not* his daughter."

"No. I'm not," I agree. "But me and your dad, I think we're just friends."

She shakes her head again. "No you're not. He

thinks you're pwetty, I can tell. He's never wooked at anyone wike you. I think you're pwetty, too. And you're nice." She shrugs, swinging the end of the rope back and forth, her hair in two Cindy Lou Who pigtails on top of her head, and I wonder, did Price do her hair? The image of his ridiculously large, thick, calloused fingers being able to do something so delicate has a clutch starting again down in my belly. Hailey cocks her head on a nod like she's come to a decision on something important, then says, "I wouldn't mind if you mawwied him. You'd have my bwessing."

I hesitate, then reach up and pinch her chin softly. "Thanks. I wouldn't mind, either." I force a smile I'm not feeling. "But right now, you need to teach me how to climb this rope. I don't want to be the only one at camp that can't do it."

She laughs and nods, her little face spreading in a much more genuine smile than my own, and I wish I could give her a more certain answer.

Kids.

Jesus. They have a way of making complicated things sound so easy. Marry Price, be Hailey's stepmom, live happily ever after.

But life isn't a fairytale.

Price would probably shrivel up and die in the city, with honking taxis and all the concrete and lack of nature. He'd look ridiculous in a suit and tie, sitting behind a desk, where adventure would consist of a walk in the park or eighteen holes of golf. No, this is his natural habitat and where he belongs.

And as for me?

I tell myself that I have a master's program to attend. I have a life mapped out. Goals set.

Hailey gives me pointers on how to climb the rope as she scurries up, reminding me of how Price tackled that rope over the wall a minute ago.

They both belong out here. I'm just suddenly not sure where I belong.

Chapter Ten

Price

"Don't you dare hurt her."
I turn away from watching Summer with Hailey at the ropes, to find her friend Dolly glaring at me, one hand on her cocked hip.

"You're supposed to be watching the kids in your group," I growl.

She laughs mockingly. "So are you." Even so, she glances over her shoulder. "They're fine. There's another counselor with them. Daniel happily stepped in when I said I had to take a break."

"Daniel..." I frown.

She rolls her eyes. "Daniel Goodman. Don't you

know the names of the other counselors here? He's good with the kids, and they like him."

"What do you want, Dolly?"

"Don't think I don't see the way you're looking at Summer. She might be naive, but I'm not. The only reason she came here was to have a last blowout before she goes off to New York in the fall. She wanted to lose her V card, and you've helped her with that. Congratulations. But it was always going to be a no strings deal." Her eyes soften as she glances from me to Summer, then back again. "Look, she's my best friend, and she has a life waiting for her. A good career, probably a sensible marriage. Two point four kids. The whole deal. Please don't take that away from her. The romance of summer fades quickly. Especially out here, for a girl like her."

* * *

The contract taunts me from the desk, the blank signature box mocking my sudden inability to make a decision. It was supposed to be simple. This was what I wanted. What Ted wanted.

The plan was perfect.

I try to tell myself that it's the best for me. The best for Hailey. The best for Summer.

So why am I hovering?

I re-read the legal clauses again, remembering how the exec from the TV company drilled the essential rules into me and the extra clause about *fraternization,* of all things.

"No hookups. No booze. No BS. This isn't MTV. We want you squeaky clean, Mr. Webber, and we're willing to pay well to ensure that, but if you step out of line we're going to have to cut you off. NO relationships. Ratings will plummet if the female audience doesn't have the fantasy that you're available."

A week ago, I would have signed on the dotted line while he stood there, regardless of how much I sort of dislike the whole corporate structure of network entertainment.

Instead, I insisted that I needed time to go over the details and have my lawyer give it a once over. Utter bullshit, one rule broken already. I don't even have a fucking lawyer, and I'm pretty sure I understand enough to know this is a once in a lifetime deal.

My own show, with Ted and the camp I want to call home.

Total reality, nothing fake, no airbrushing for the cameras. Apparently, the single dad angle is hot right now. That whole thing about the female demographic wanting the fantasy they could be with me, whatever the fuck that means. I know what it means for me: the freedom to do things my way. Raise my daughter where I can keep her safe.

The only catch?

No women. Part of what they're selling is how I've

sworn off relationships to raise my daughter the old-fashioned way, with an appreciation for nature and a healthy sense of adventure. As a result, I'm agreeing to stay single for six seasons. If I'm caught with anyone, especially at camp, I forfeit the entire contract.

"I can't fucking do this," I mutter to myself, slamming my fist down on the desk in a fit of rage.

All I'm seeing in my mind is the way Summer and Hailey looked so happy playing on the ropes. The way Hailey instructed Summer how to climb them, and the way she clapped and laughed like crazy when Summer made it halfway to the top.

How Summer felt wrapped around my dick. Calling me daddy, for fuck sake.

How can I ruin that?

A smile creases my lips at the memory. Am I really about to sign all that away?

But then, what about what Dolly told me? Summer doesn't want this. She has a life waiting for her, and it sounds like an amazing one. How selfish would I have to be to take that away from her? Not to mention Ted's investment in this place, which was kind of predicated on me doing the whole TV deal. Camp WanderLust has been losing money for years, and if it goes down, so does he.

With a growl, I push the contract away. I need to think, and I can't do that sitting behind a desk. My mind isn't programmed that way.

I need sky above me, dirt under my feet, and the smell of pine trees and a little danger.

But what does Summer need?

Chapter Eleven

Summer

"What'd that asshole do?" Dolly crosses the cabin from the door, grabbing me by the arms. "I'm going to fucking kill him. I told him not to hurt you or he'd have to deal with me. Guess he made his choice. Spill, girl."

She tugs me down to sit on the edge of my cot next to her. I'm shaking my head, trying to find the words through the tears that now won't stop.

"It's not his fault," I manage, looking down to see I've broken two more nails.

My knee burns where I skinned it falling off the end of the rope after Hailey went to eat with the other kids and I got a wild hair thinking I was some big adventurer and could climb all the way to the top.

"The hell it isn't. He looking for free babysitting in the form of a new stepmom for his kid? I fucking knew he was going to try—"

"No!" I splutter, swiping the back of my hand over my wet cheeks. "No, he doesn't want me. He has this amazing life planned. Out here, in this crazy world that makes no sense to me with all the spiders and bears and....*stuff*. I should never have come here."

I draw back, my legs needing to move as I start to pace the small counselors' area of the cabin. My stuff is scattered everywhere. What the hell was I thinking, bringing fucking bath bombs to camp?

None of what I am makes sense here.

"I have to go, Dolly. Will you tell him I quit? I can't. I just want to go. I'm sorry about our wild summer. I should have known this was not going to be my jam."

"Wait, what? You don't quit things. You've never quit anything in your life, including when I dragged you to auto shop as your sophomore elective. You did *that*. Talk to me."

I draw a deep breath, expanding my lungs until they feel like they'll burst, bending down to pick up my pink velour Betsy Johnson tracksuit and shove it into my suitcase. "He hasn't said anything. I went looking for him. More like snooping for him... I shouldn't have, but I went in his office. It wasn't locked..." I try to justify the unjustifiable invasion. "I wanted to talk, I mean, we needed to talk. I started poking around and there was a contract. For the TV network. With a big clause that forbids him from having any sort of relationship during the length of the contract."

The sounds of kids squealing outside and my racing heartbeat muffle everything else.

"But you don't want a relationship. Do you? Just a summer fling..."

I shrug. "Right. No. I don't know!" I hiss in frustration. "I... Ugggg." I groan. "I don't fit in here with spiders and dirt and everything, but, I like it. I love Hailey, I love the air, the thrill, I love... I'm *in love* with Price. I could see myself living like this, with him, but it doesn't matter. Even if he wanted something with me, clearly he can't have it."

The tears come no matter how hard I fight, and I can't take it anymore. I throw the tube of toothpaste I was packing down onto the bed, and run, ignoring her pleas for me to stop. The cabin is too close, there isn't enough air. I need be outside, so I run. I'm not even a running type of girl, but right now my legs are carrying me away, away, away.

I head for the lake. I've never been in a lake before. I was always too scared there were fish in there and what if the bottom was slimy?

As I catch sight of the water, doubt and confusion hurdle around inside me. I want to dive in the dark water and let it swallow me, so I don't have to think or feel or wonder about what I should or shouldn't do here.

I'm so out of my element with these crazy feelings.

I stop, leaning forward, bracing my arms on my bent knees, then stand straight, unclipping the green metal clip from my belt, cocking back to throw it into the water.

"What are you going to do?" I whisper-ask myself, my arm frozen, ready to throw the strange but emotional gift into the dark water but the silence is broken with footsteps from behind me.

It's gotta be Dolly.

A hand encases my upper arm, squeezing. Hard.

Dolly's been working out, I think as I turn, and I find myself face to chest with *him*.

"What are you...?" I glance around, but we're alone, and he's definitely not been chasing me down. His breathing is calm and steady but the set of his chin and the way he's hollowing his cheeks makes him look more intense than usual. "How did you find me?"

"I was about to ask you the same thing. How'd you know where I was?"

"I didn't..." I shake my head, as he tugs my arm down, pressing the carabiner back into my palm and closing my fingers around the cool aluminum. I'm overcome again with his size and the odd comfort I feel when I'm close to him, even in the midst of so much uncertainty and overwhelming emotions. Not to mention, the idea that what we did last night could be creating something inside me right now.

Price grunts, a muscle in his cheek ticks. "Then why

were you running? What were you going to do with that? You shouldn't be out here alone."

"I was running because I wanted to and I was...never mind. I shouldn't be *here* at all. Here, I mean, in all this," The certainty in my voice falters as I think of how I called him Daddy. How he called himself Daddy. What was I thinking? That was a bit over the top for a girl's first time, right?

Then why did it feel so good?

"Doesn't matter. We're going to talk." The words come out stuttering and stalled, like he's forcing them out of his throat. "I hate talking, but with you, it's all I seem to want to do."

I raise my eyebrows for a second and he rolls his eyes.

"Okay, that's not the only thing, but it's something I've never wanted to do with anyone else."

I release a sardonic chuckle, feeling the tears start to sting the corners of my eyes again. "It's okay. I get it. Let's *not* talk. I'm tired of talking. I don't want to hear you say we can't be together. You were straight with me from the beginning, and I'm just a stupid, stupid girl."

"Don't *ever* call yourself stupid," he growls, his massive hands resting on the sides of my head, encasing me with their power as I squeeze the metal clip in my hand.

His gaze makes my heart thunder. It's like being trapped by a mountain lion, one that's decided I'm his next meal. And I'm too confused to fight it.

"Don't *ever* put yourself down," he repeats. "You're perfect. Too perfect. I have no right to ask anything of you, my Daisy, but I'm going to anyway, because I can't imagine a future without you in it. I love you, baby. Like, *love you*, love you, you get it?"

I open my mouth, then hesitate as I catch sight of a tiny movement on the top of his shoulder. I squint, knowing instantly what's coming.

Heat blasts through me, but for once, it's not fear, it's just... annoyance.

I clip the carabiner back on my belt loop on a huff.

I'm annoyed at the spider crawling down the sleeve of Price's gray t-shirt, but I'm more annoyed at my own naiveté about summer flings and no strings.

Seems there's no such thing.

I reach up and flick the black creeper off his arm, watching it fly in an arc through the air, then cross my arms. A crow caws in the distance as I throw it all out there. "What about the TV deal? That's sort of a non-starter for a relationship. I saw how much they're offering you, Price, it's a lot. I saw the...no *fraternization* clause."

"And it doesn't mean a fucking thing if I don't have you. I know you have plans too. Dolly told me. I'm ready to fit in with them. Me and Hailey. It will be a different kind of adventure, but one I want more than all the ones that came before. Whatever you want, we'll make it work. I'll get a job as a fucking bank teller. I don't care, none of it means anything if you aren't with us."

I shake my head, turning up my hands. "You said you would never let Hailey grow up in the city. She's happy here."

He winces, as if at some deep pain. "She's happy with me. And she's happy when she's with you. I'll figure it out. I'll keep you both safe, even if it means I never let you out of my sight. I... I don't know. All I know is that I can't be without you. And I can't take away the things you want in your life."

I watch him struggling to reconcile his own needs and what he wants for his daughter, and suddenly it all becomes clear.

What am I even crying for?

"You said you love me," I say in a kind of daze, and he nods. A smile starts to tickle at the corners of my lips, and I wipe at my drying eyes, his massive hands still clutching my head like he's afraid I might fly away somewhere. "You love me?"

"I love you, Summer. Daisy. Little Sis. Baby. All of you. I know it doesn't make sense, but I live on instinct and my instincts have never been wrong."

"And you don't care about the TV deal?"

"I'll tear up the contract in an instant if you just say the word. I'll find a way to pay Ted back for his investment in me and this place. There's more than one network out there. Shit, I've had all sorts of companies after me for endorsements for years. I always thought it was a sell out to do that, but I see it differently now. I'm not poor by any means, but I made promises. I'll figure it all out. If I can climb my way out of a swamp in the Amazon with no compass and a broken arm, I can do this. Hailey too, she's toughened me up in ways I didn't know I needed to be tough. I can take on anything, even living in a city. With her. With you. None of it means anything without you. You've made me want a different life. A life I never imagined before you."

"So, you don't need to take Hailey to the city. Because I'm staying here."

He frowns. "What?"

"If you'll have me?" I slide my hands around the hard muscle of his waist, his hands dropping to grab me by my ass, tugging me upward, mounted on the front of him like a baby in one of those chest carriers.

"You're not giving up your dreams, but I got you, baby. Daddy will always be here for you."

He'll never let me go, never let me fall.

I didn't think I wanted a life of adventure, but with him behind me, beside me or on top of me, it will be the safest adventure of all time.

"Dolly's gonna kill me," he murmurs into my ear, before planting a kiss on that magical spot on my neck, my skin rippling all the way down to my toes. "She told me if I ruined you, I'd have her to deal with."

"Better make the ruining worth it then, don't you think?" I say with a grin, rolling my hips against him, working the bottom of my t-shirt up and over my head. "Let's live dangerously."

Chapter Twelve

Summer

Epilogue...seven years later...

My husband has made some adjustments when it comes to his version of 'roughing it'.

Electricity, four bedrooms and six bathrooms, a library, offices for both of us, a playroom for the kids and an all-white kitchen with every gadget and gourmet appliance Price could convince the delivery drivers to bring all the way up here make our mountain 'cabin' something we can both live with.

He's just outside, torso glistening in the summer sun as he swings the ax in an enormous arc, bringing it down with a 'crack' onto the standing piece of wood, splintering it into three pieces.

Our oldest outside of Hailey is Nick, named after Price's brother, and he just turned five last month. He's his father's little shadow. My heart strains when I see how he looks at Price like he created fire.

He's an amazing father to all three of our babies. I adopted Hailey officially the day after our wedding, having another type of ceremony to symbolize bringing our family together officially.

That was all Price's idea. The big lug has the biggest heart.

I shiver as his stunning green eyes shift, eating me up as he looks over to see me standing in the doorway of the cabin, wearing a white lace-trimmed eyelet nightgown, cradling my steaming cup of coffee and taking in the beauty of our surroundings.

The old cabin where we spent our first night together sits about a hundred yards from this newer one. We use it still as a getaway, and love to re-create our 'only one bed' night as often as we can.

My husband wants to be inside of me every chance he gets, and I admit I still tease and taunt him, not that he needs any encouragement in that department.

He is always thinking of what's best for me, even when I don't like it.

I've had more than one red bottom in our time together, but after the spanking comes the orgasms. So. Many. Orgasms.

Those early days of playing our big brother, little sister roles have grown into their own naughty fantasies. But that's just for play time.

The other title I use for my husband is Daddy. More than just a turn-on during sexy times, it's who he is with me. Protective, nurturing, a bit bossy but always with a reason and a guiding hand showing me the way.

Out of the corner of my eye, I see movement and turn, wondering if it's Electra showing up again to show off her newest cub, but no, it's the camera crew here to change out and adjust some of the cameras that hang in some of the rooms of the cabin.

As the three men exit their van, Hailey comes running out from the woods, sticks stuck in her hair, holding up what looks like a six-foot snakeskin to add to her collection.

She raises it toward Price, with a big smile and he drops into a crouch, giving her all his attention while she displays her newest treasure. She's the original wild child for sure, and she's so much like her Daddy that sometimes I feel outnumbered by their sheer ability to navigate the wilderness that surrounds our home.

Me? I am still not a fan of spiders, but I'll re-home them back outside when Hailey or Price are not around.

"Ma'am." The tallest of the crew approaches, and I

nod, then shrink back a step, remembering I'm still in my nightgown with nothing on under it and I don't wish harm to come to the innocent camera crew, but I might be too late. They all three take a long look at me before I can stop what I know is about to happen.

In a split second, Price has Hailey corralled to watch Nick, and he's halfway to the unsuspecting three men when I throw out a Hail Mary to save them.

"Come! Inside, there's a huge, hairy, ten-inch spider! *Hurry!*" I scurry back into the foyer, sneaking a quick look back outside where Price pauses for a beat, his eyes flicking from the crew to the house, then back and forth one more time before he lets out a curse, pointing at the three men.

"Don't look at her. That's all mine," he grumbles but leaves them standing, stomping toward the cabin.

We have a new spinoff series starting in a few weeks. Reality TV has become part of our life, but we keep normalcy as well with months off and certain parts of our life is off limits.

Price barges through the door, shirtless, hands balled into fists, stalling as I stand with my back against the wall in the hall.

"Where's the spider?" He swivels his head around, searching, as I shrug my shoulders, clicking my teeth together on an apologetic smile.

"There's no spider," I admit as he releases a hoarse breath, his chest falling as he shakes his head. "I'm sorry,

I didn't want the children to see you breaking those men's arms and legs. So traumatic for them."

His long fingers move to scratch at his forehead, then rake through the waves of his chestnut brown hair. His features have deepened, ruddy and masculine and my desire for him grows with each passing year.

He's in front of me in a second and I lower my coffee mug onto the chair next to me, then run a finger down the indent of his chest. "Maybe I just needed some attention."

I can already feel the blush warming my cheeks at the lusty look in his eyes.

"Wife." He grunts, chest heaving up and down. "You test me."

"You love it," I tease on a smirk as I use my other hand to work the buttons open on my nightgown, but I'm not even to the second one before I'm swept off my feet with a yelp, carried over his shoulder down the hall, my wetness already slippery between my legs at the thought of what's coming.

Me, for one.

I do crave my husband. So much. More than when we met, I think, and he feels the same way. The first years were so busy with the camp and the baby, the reality show and me working through my master's program.

Price and I tried keeping a place in New York at first for me to do my studies at NYU. He put in the effort, but in the end, Hailey was miserable in the city.

Our wild child longed for the forest and the bugs and all the creatures and peace it brings her. In the end, I realized the things I loved about the city could be had in short bursts of time, getting my fix before returning to the serenity of our life here.

I finished my degree online and take on a few local clients when it works into the schedule. I don't need to work, but I like what I do. I like helping and language and giving people a voice that have struggled is fulfilling in a way I need outside of taking care of my brood.

Price flips me down onto my feet, fisting my hair and driving me to my knees before reaching out with his other hand and swinging the door closed, flipping the lock as heat prickles over my skin.

He's got that look in his eyes that tells me things might get a little rough, but that only urges me on.

"Daddy wants me to help him relax?" I tease, my hands already on his belt, slipping the leather from the buckle, his enormous erection popping free as soon as I work the button and zipper on his jeans.

"Suck," he says in that low, throaty voice that makes my insides all gooey. "No more talking. Get to work."

I do as I'm told, greedily taking him between my lips, sighing at the first taste of his flesh, the little bead of pre-cum lighting up my taste buds.

My husband takes, but he gives so much more. He gave me the fairytale wedding of my dreams, with all the lace and flowers any girly girl could want.

Introducing him to my parents was a lot for them at first. He's not the sort of man they probably thought I would take to, as well as our age difference and the fact that he had a daughter. It took them a minute to get settled into it all. But they saw how happy I am, and although they enjoy their visits here, they are keeping their condo in the city, which works out. The kids and I can get our taste of the other side of life whenever we want.

The camp is thriving. The WanderLust Love Adventure reality show is in its fourth season. It's a more popular spinoff that happened when Price told the producers in no uncertain terms that he was definitely going to *fraternize* with me.

They came up with a new idea, sort of a Fantasy Island, Love Boat and Survivor mash up. It took off like a rocket, although we have to keep the kids clear of the camp when things start to heat up between some of the couples.

Dolly runs the business side of the TV show, and she and Ted ended up doing some fraternizing of their own, and have been living their own adventure together for the past few years.

"You're so beautiful with my cock in your mouth," Price growls from above as I struggle with his length. "Do a good job. I'm going to have a go at that pussy of yours too."

It doesn't take long before he fills my throat with his

warm, savory flavor. Then the tables are turned, and his mouth is on me.

"The crew is waiting," I whimper as his tongue pushes into my opening and I nearly go off right there.

"They can wait. I want them to smell me on you, and you on me. They need to know this is all mine."

He dives back in and the orgasms start to flow. His mouth is exchanged for his magical cock as the scent of our sex warms the air.

"I love you, Daddy," I whisper as he braces his body over me, gliding in and out, his face in a twisted grimace. Those words always push him to the edge.

"I love you too, baby," he says as he pumps inside of me.

His mouth comes down to meet mine as his warmth spreads inside of me and another orgasm has me crying out in pleasure.

"You are my sun and my moon," Price whispers into my ear as he collapses on top of me. "My earth and stars."

"And you are my rock and my foundation. My path and my guide. My love. My world," I say back as he brushes a hand down my arm, twining our fingers together.

Above the bed hanging in a small shadow box in the center of a menagerie of photos from our wedding, and milestones from our lives, is that chipped green metal gift he gave me all those years ago. It's served us well, holding us together through all the adventures of life.

Price's voice is warm and breathy in my ear, "My wife. Mine. All fucking mine."

Want to see his stick?
Yeah, yeah ya do. Grab it here!

TEMPING THE KING

She's an overachiever with control issues. He's the king of chaos with no room in his life for love.

Hockey players make the worst clients ever.

They're arrogant neanderthals, who are completely out of touch with their emotions. But, that's exactly where I come in.

See, I'm a professional cuddler and when the Detroit Blades hockey team has a problem, they send it my way.

Taking on another player is the last thing I want to do, but the deal is too sweet to turn down, so I'm stuck with one last grumpy, angry ice warrior named King Hertzog.

Big. Mistake.

With one platonic touch, he becomes obsessed with claiming me as his own and his caveman antics upend my perfectly ordered life.

I've always been in charge, but all of the sudden, when King says kneel, I find myself looking up into the icy eyes of the man that makes my insides melt and my heart hope for things it shouldn't.

But, when I have to make a choice between family and love, will all our dreams come crashing down? Or, will we score the winning goal?

TEMPTING THE KING NOW AVAILABLE

Amz Banned - It's yours for free!

But, wait! Before you go...
Amazon
BANNED
EARNING HER KEEP! So, I'll give it to you free!
Get it here FREE!

Amz Banned - It's yours for free!

Dani wrote some other books...

FIND ALL MY OTHER BOOKS

HERE

Let's Stay Connected!

FOLLOW ME ON FACEBOOK
FACEBOOK FRIENDS
GOODREADS: Dani Wyatt
PRIVATE READER'S GROUP: Wyatt's Wenches
Dani Wyatt on Amazon
dani@daniwyatt.com
www.daniwyatt.com

Find your tribe...
Join Dani's Private Facebook Group

About Dani

Dani Wyatt used to feel bad about having such dirty thoughts. Luckily, one day, she decided to start writing them down. Her ultra-obsessed, alpha heroes have a wicked possessive streak and an insatiable libido. Her heroines are intelligent, quirky, and worry about having too much muffin top. So, if you like your insta-love over the top, super-hot, and always a happily ever after, you're in the right place.

She's fighting middle age like a warrior and lives an average life battling gravity. When she's not writing, she is probably laughing about some irony (like the fact that A-1 Steak Sauce is vegan), reading, riding her horse, or looking cross-eyed at some piece of technology sent to ruin her day.

Thank you.

About Dani

I have so many amazing people I've met since I started putting my
naughty thoughts on the page. To some of the first fans who supported me, the bloggers,
fellow authors who have been more than generous with their
time and opinions, as well as the other professionals that put up with my particular kind of crazy, thank you.
...you guys remind me every day that when we support each other, everyone wins.

xoxoxo